OVERSEER'S WOMAN

Yvonne Hilton

YVONNE HILTON

outskirts
press

CHAPTER 1

*T*he black man's screams tore up the fabric of the morning. Raw and much too high for any man's voice, they pierced the thin air with awful shrieks that seemed to go on forever.

"What yuh want is t' git a good set o' stripes on him. Yah?"

The white man doing the whipping, Thomas Van Roop, had once been the quartermaster on a Dutch merchant ship and had done his fair share of floggings. He had a strong right arm and the arc of his whip cut the air, making rhythmic cracks each time the separate straps ripped into the black man's bare back. With each lash, a new gash tore open that spurted thick, dark blood. Van Roop was instructing a white youngster, standing a short distance behind him and who was steadily backing away from the scene, his heavy shoes crunching the scattered stones and pebbles that littered the clearing.

"Pay no attention t' his noise. They allus holler like that. Yuh got t' git used t' it if yuh ever hope t' become the new overseer on one o' Reverend Van Driessen's farms. This one, Peter, well, he's tried t' run two times already. Yah? It sets a bad example fer the others if we let him git away wit' such."

Van Roop had a thick, Dutch accent that his years in the Colony of New York had done little to alter. As usual, whenever he was teaching something really important, his voice became gentle, as though he were explaining the correct method for shoeing a horse. The runner being lashed, whose name was Peter, was getting the full measure of punishment – thirty-nine lashes with a special cat-o-nine-tails; each tail was studded with sharp bits of metal. His suffering was meant to serve as a lesson and a warning to the other enslaved men and women who had been assembled to witness – and learn from this example of severe punishment. They stood gathered in knots, their heads bowed and eyes averted from the scene. Peter was one of them, a field worker, even though he'd only been with them on the farm for a month. The truth was, he'd actually been purchased about six months earlier but, on the first night of his arrival, he'd escaped by slipping through an opening in the back wall of the shack where the unmarried male workers were housed. He was captured a week later and got his first whipping from Van Roop, who had delivered what he considered a decent beating.

But Peter knew how to take a whipping; at the first stroke, he began roaring and kept it up until he'd convinced the overseer that he'd gotten the point of the painful lesson. Soon afterward, Peter had run again, this time staying free for more than three months, despite slave catchers combing the countryside the entire time. He was finally caught again when a farmer's wife discovered him raiding her hen house. This time, Van Roop decided to use the cat-o-nine-tails from his sea-faring days; after twenty lashes, it left a man scarred for life.

The youngster, called Martin Tucker, was just sixteen and had no stomach for this brutal task he was expected to learn. He could almost feel each high-pitched scream tear through him. Even though he was Van Roop's apprentice and, expected to eventually take on the job of overseer, just thinking about whipping the slaves turned his stomach. He didn't believe he would ever be able to inflict so much pain on anyone, at least he didn't think so on that day.

At the thirty-ninth lash, Van Roop at last let his right arm drop to his side. He undid the kerchief around his neck with his other hand, and wiped his face with the cloth, then, motioned for two men to untie Peter from the whipping post and throw a bucket of water on him; by the thirtieth lash, Peter had finally fainted and Van Roop wanted him revived.

"One a' yuh go on an fetch Lucy. Yah? Tell her t' git her salves an some cloths ready fer his back."

Lucy, the black woman Van Roop sent for, knew how to clean and bind up wounds so they wouldn't fester. After his severe flogging, Peter would need tending day and night to survive. Each slave on the farm was worth far too much money to be allowed to die.

Four black men lifted Peter and carried him, face down, toward Lucy's shack in the slaves' quarters. From her place at the back of one group of women, she wordlessly followed the grim procession. By now, Peter was awake and moaning, and soon enough, he would be screaming again, once Lucy began to clean his wounds with warm salt water, which was used to draw out infection and debris.

Van Roop turned to Martin and taking note of young Tucker's greenish color, he laughed, "Yuh think me a harsh man, do yuh? Mark my words, I done that Peter a great favor. Yah? Now he'll behave like a proper worker. 'N fact, one 'o these days, he'll come t' be yer mos loyal man. Them that runs, they's the ones got t' be broken in hard, like I jus' done."

Tucker could only stare at Van Roop. Most of the time, he tried to accept the overseer's reasoning for his system of punishments and rewards. For instance, a slave's insistence that he was too sick to work a full day would be acknowledged only once for that particular slave and Van Roop might even allow him to leave the field early. But after that, never again could that man claim illness without risking a whipping. "Else they all gits lazy. Yah?"

Tucker understood the concept, even as he could see how the policy pushed sick men out into the fields all too often. He frequently spent fruitless hours trying to reconcile his own discomfort with this and other examples of the delicate balance involved in controlling the large numbers of slaves needed to work such a vast, almost 50,000 acre farm as this one.

The Hudson Valley in Colonial New York had many farms of 50,000 acres or more, plantations really, as well as much smaller tenant-run farms, all of which supplied food and other crops to the cities of Albany and New Paltz. Many of these large farms belonged to wealthy absentee owners who lived on their main estates just outside one city or the other. For that reason, owners would employ overseers to live full-time on the farm and run it. Frequently this overseer was the only white person on the farm, and he often had responsibility for as many as 100 black slaves. Peter and Lucy lived on such a farm, just one of several, owned by the Reverend Petrus Van Driessen, a prominent minister whose main residence was an estate near Albany.

Just before sundown, on the day of Peter's whipping, young Martin Tucker was supposed to be helping Van Roop supervise the end of the slaves' workday. They were cultivating four fields and in each one, the overseer would blow a horn indicating that work could stop for the day. Van Roop had given Tucker that task in two of the more distant fields, and the youngster blew his horn when the sun was still fairly high above the horizon. The men and women within earshot, each bent over rows of young corn shoots, clearing away weeds and other choking growths, straightened up in amazement that the signal was coming so early. Within minutes, the field was empty. Tucker repeated this early signal in the next field and soon found himself alone. Making certain there was no one to see him, he then took the same path the slaves used to get to their quarters.

Tucker wasn't sure where he was headed, or even why he'd stopped the workers so early, but he thought he heard a faint sound carried on the wind that he simply had to investigate. He let his ears and his feet guide him along the dirt path through a thicket of young trees and low bushes until he reached the first of the workers' shacks. Now, he could hear the sound more clearly; it was a steady, almost rhythmic screaming coming from that first shack.

The door was closed but there was no latch; Tucker pushed it open, then stood in the doorway, transfixed. Peter, the runner, who had been so severely flogged, lay facedown and lengthwise on a wooden table in the center of the room; his entire upper body, hips and thighs rested on the table, while his lower legs were suspended.

At the head of the table, Lucy stood holding a basin and a rag, by turns dipping the rag in the basin, soaking it, and then squeezing the liquid into each open gash on Peter's back. All the while she worked, she kept murmuring to him, "Just go on an holler. Just holler with the pain. That's right. Holler loud as you need to."

Peter had gripped Lucy's skirt at both hips and might have gotten hold of her flesh as well, that's how tight his fists were on either side of her. He'd rammed the top of his head into her stomach and, with each pass of the soaked rag across his back, he let loose a scream that came from deep in the center of his being. The ropy veins in his neck bulged and deflated with each scream's rise and ebb.

Tucker knew for certain that, if Van Roop found out he'd let the workers off early and where he was right now, he'd find himself on the business end of one of the overseer's several implements of punishment. Van Roop had no compunction about hitting Tucker, either with the butt of his short whip or the small club that he carried on his waistband. Indeed, the overseer considered the judicious application of corporal punishment part of his responsibility in training the young man.

But despite the potential consequences, Tucker couldn't tear himself away. Watching Lucy's deft movements and Peter's agony triggered powerful quivering sensations in parts of his body that he'd become intensely aware of for some time now, and which he was unable to fully control. He never heard the crunch of footsteps behind him and was shocked when Van Roop yanked him backward out of the doorway and delivered a blow to his head that knocked the young man flat on the ground.

"Figgered I'd find yuh here. Shirkin' yer duties, yah?" Van Roop voice didn't sound particularly angry.

Tucker sat up, rubbing the throbbing spot. Van Roop's club had managed to scatter every cogent thought in his head. He struggled to his feet and stood before the overseer, fully expecting further punishment.

"That's all. I ain't gone do nothin' else t' yuh. Natural t' be curious what happens after a whippin' like yuh seen today. Yah?"

It wasn't that Tucker had never watched Van Roop whip the slaves. In fact, the overseer administered such punishment whenever he deemed it absolutely necessary. But, as he'd carefully point out to young Tucker on each occasion, one had to weigh the severity of the offense and be ready to use less extreme measures whenever possible.

"Besides, yuh got t' learn t' use the lash proper. Else yuh maim what ain't yourn and yuh be bound t' pay the owner. An, if'n yuh kills one by mistake, the owner will take the full cost o that slave out a yer wages. Yah?

Van Roop even had Tucker practice applying the whip to the tree trunk in front of the cabin they shared. Under the overseer's watchful eye, the young man learned to snap it at just the right angle so the lash curling against the trunk would take off only enough bark to barely reveal the white wood beneath. On a man's–or a woman's bare back, it was important not to cut too deeply, but rather to leave the kinds of scars that reminded the offender not to risk such behavior again.

Martin Tucker was the fifth boy in a family of thirteen children. With so many mouths to feed, his father, an itinerate tailor, had to spend endless hours sewing in order to earn barely enough to keep his family fed and sheltered. The man rented a workbench in the rear of a small shop owned by a more established tailor. The only way he had been able make ends meet was to turn each of his sons out to fend for himself, as soon as the child was old enough to learn a trade.

Martin was only twelve when his father sent him to the Reverend Van Driessen's church with instructions to "make yerself useful fer free till he decides what t' do with ya." Even though the Tucker family was Anglican, and therefore didn't attend the Dutch Reform Church of which the reverend was senior pastor, everyone in Albany knew that, if you sent a boy to Reverend Van Driessen, the gentleman would find an appropriate situation for him.

The lad sat for almost a full day in the drafty church vestibule while the good reverend conducted ecclesiastical business, which seemed to consist of endless interviews with one congregant after another. These were all white men, well-turned-out councilmen, aldermen and merchants, as well as rough-dressed farmers and laborers. Finally, as the supper hour was approaching, young Martin heard his name being called by the clerk, who was seated on a stool at a tall writing desk just outside the reverend's office.

"Tucker," called out the clerk, a rather dried-up stick of a man. He peered down at the boy through the pince-nez perched almost on the end of his long hooked nose. "Is that you?"

"Yessir. 'Tis me," Martin replied stoutly, trying to stand a bit straighter. Because he'd grown so much taller than the other boys his age, the lad's father would always have to remind him not to slouch. Now, since he realized it might benefit him to try to appear grown-up, he squared his shoulders while nervously shifting from one hand to the other the bundle containing all his belongings.

"The Reverend will see you now." The clerk gestured in the general vicinity of the office and then immediately went back to whatever he'd been doing.

For a full minute, Martin didn't move. In his mind, the youngster was trying to come up with an accurate description of the clerk to entertain his brothers and sisters with whenever he saw them again. But, having never learned to read or write and so, lacking the vocabulary, the best he could manage was "Dry Bones."

He was completely startled when a booming voice sang out from the office.

"Tucker, Martin Tucker. Where are you lad?"

"Right here, Sir!" The boy replied, hurrying in the direction of the voice.

"So, my boy, I understand you seek work. What can you do?"

"Anything ya set me to, Sir. I'm a hard worker. My father says so." Martin added, "I can work fer free if'n ya don't have nothing y'can pay me fer right now."

Reverend Van Driessen studied the lad closely for several minutes. He'd mastered the art of sizing up the boys who came to him. There was always a need for lads with quick minds but most of the ones who presented themselves had only strong backs and were little better than his Negro slaves.

The Reverend had been one of the leading citizens of Albany since arriving in the Colony in 1712. Now, after some 27 years, he'd amassed a sizeable fortune, along with ownership of four farms. Three of them he'd leased to tenant farmers, but on the fourth and most productive one, he'd employed Thomas Van Roop as overseer. In this way, the Reverend could be sure of getting the most work out of the slaves on this farm. Van Roop had been in his employ for 20 years now and it was time for him to give the man an apprentice.

The Reverend was a man tall enough to carry his comfortable girth without appearing fat. He rose and came from behind his ornately carved desk. Gesturing expansively with one large fleshy hand, he said, "Well young Tucker, how'd you like to work under my man out on one of my farms? Have you ever done farm work?"

Martin had never even seen a farm; his entire world had consisted of the narrow city lane where his family lived crowded into a two-room hovel. He had only a vague idea of what such a place might be like and no idea of what work he'd be expected to do. He responded honestly: "Sir, I ain't never done no farm work but I can learn it."

"Good enough," the Reverend responding, returning to his desk, "Go home and get your things together. Be ready to leave at first light tomorrow. You'll be apprenticed to the overseer so there'll be no pay, but you will have room and board."

Thus, the matter was settled. Martin explained that he had no need to return home since he had everything with him already. Reverend Van Driessen allowed him to spend the night in the parsonage kitchen, which was adjacent to the church, and even sent one of his house slaves out with a bit of supper for the lad. Early the next morning, Martin boarded a wagon loaded with provisions and headed out of Albany, not realizing that this would be the last time he would ever see the city.

Before young Tucker left, the Reverend did give him a much abbreviated description of work being done on the farm that was going to be his new home. "We raise wheat, corn, rye and oats. Sheep for wool and mutton, as well as a good stock of cattle, both for beef and milk. Got an excellent mill too. Oh, and ninety-eight adult slaves: ninety-six field workers and two millers."

By the time the provision wagon reached the farm, the trip had taken the better part of the morning. Tucker learned that the four men doing the driving were called teamsters. Their job was to bring merchandise and supplies from the city to the various farms belonging to Reverend Van Driessen. The teamsters ordered the youth to get down and help them unload the wagon. Tucker promptly did as he was told. As they were about to begin working, a tall, gaunt man approached.

"How come I gotta tell yuh every time t' take them provisions where they supposed t' go an not just leave em wherever yuh want? Yah?" the man shouted. "Albert!" he addressed the head teamster directly, "I swear, yer the laziest goddamn fool ever was born!"

Martin's heart jumped when the man started yelling. He immediately put back the bolt of burlap he'd just dragged off the wagon. The others, including Albert seemed more or less unfazed. They did, however, reload the wagon and follow the gaunt man for another quarter mile to a huge building adjacent to a stream.

Here, black men and women moved about doing what seemed to be an endless round of tasks, none of which Martin recognized. Several of those men joined the teamsters and together they made short work of the unloading.

Martin helped out as best he could by positioning himself next to the wagon and handing the man nearest him whatever bundle he could grab the fastest. Eventually, the work was done and the black men vanished, or so it seemed to Martin. He found himself standing alone beside the empty wagon. Looking around, he noticed the gaunt man walking away, closely followed by all the teamsters. Then the man turned abruptly to Martin and gestured for him to come along.

It seemed they were headed to the tall, gaunt man's house, a split-log cabin located at the end of a road on a hill. Once there, everyone followed him inside and took seats on the two long benches on either side of the table that dominated the room. All the earlier acrimony seemed to have been forgotten as the man pulled out two earthenware jugs and six mismatched cups. He poured amber liquid into each cup and pushed one toward Martin, who was perched uncomfortably on the edge of one bench.

"What's yer name, lad?" the man asked in the midst of a big swallow.

"Tucker, sir. Martin Tucker. I been told I'm yer new…," Martin couldn't remember the fancy word the Reverend had used to describe his new job.

"Apprentice?" the man suggested, fixing the lad with a suddenly steely stare.

"Yessir," Martin said, his voice quavering. By now, the man had frightened him thoroughly.

"Tucker, is it? How old are yuh, lad?"

"Twelve, sir"

"Well, Tucker, yuh seem a strong enough lad, so yuh should work out fine. Yah? All yuh need t' remember is, what I say goes. Yuh do whatever I tell yuh an yuh don't give me no backtalk. An, yuh take yer punishment like a man. Name's Van Roop; yer t' call me Sir. At all times. Understood?" The man's pale blue eyes never left Martin's face throughout this whole speech.

"Yessir," the lad whispered miserably, wishing suddenly he were back home with his family.

"Well, drink up, young Tucker!" Van Roop said, suddenly smiling, "Yer a man among men now."

It would be one of the very few times that Martin Tucker would witness a smile from Tomas Van Roop, and with good reason. As the youth would come to learn, for an overseer, smiling was a luxury to be indulged in rarely and only out of the sight of those who needed to fear you completely.

Three years after Peter's flogging, when Martin Tucker was nineteen, Thomas Van Roop packed his few belongings, dug up the accumulated wages he'd been burying behind the cabin he'd shared with Tucker and quit the farm. On the morning of his departure, he gave the young man a few final instructions.

"Save yer guilders, shillings an pounds. Yuh ain't gone have no place t' spend yer money anyways. Yah? 'Cause yuh can't never leave this place. If'n yuh do, time yuh git back everybody be done run off an it be on yuh t' try 'n git 'em back. Bein' a overseer's a young man's job, but it does git awful lonely. Yah? If'n they suits yer fancy, pick yuh out one 'a th' young womens t' keep yer bed warm 'n such." Van Roop had one more piece of advice. "I'm leavin' yuh the cat-o-nine tails. Yah? Yer not t' use it careless, now; yuh can kill a man too easy if'n yuh donno what yer doin'. Jes' keep it handy fer yer hardest cases."

Once Martin Tucker became overseer he, alone, had complete responsibility for keeping in line some ninety slaves working as field hands, drivers and herdsmen. Most importantly, he had to curb any tendency by the slaves to run away. This in truth meant he actually never left the farm, not even to visit a neighbor, nor could he permit any slave to leave as well.

CHAPTER 2

Sally had been born on another similar-sized Hudson Valley farm. Now age fourteen, she was one of ten slaves bought by Petrus Van Driessen II, son of the recently deceased Reverand Petrus Van Driessen. The younger Van Driessen had inherited all the farms that were part of his father's estate, and he needed additional slaves to keep them going.

Included in the purchase was Lemuel, Sally's childhood friend and lifelong love. The fact that he went with her to their new destination made it bearable to be separated from her parents and sisters. The other benefit was that, without being under her mother's watchful eye, she and Lemuel would finally be free to know each other in the Biblical sense. On the way to their new home, they had sat together in the wagon whispering their future plans and holding hands.

Lemuel was seventeen and had grownup feelings for Sally, too. He'd loved her since the age of eight when he was old enough to work the fields. Sally was this tiny girl of five, who would drag a water bucket, nearly as big as she was, out to where he'd be digging turnips or potatoes. She'd stand near his row, dipper extended, offering water to each thirsty worker. When he'd come up for his drink, she'd turn her luminous eyes in his direction and the water would taste even sweeter just because she was the one giving it. He'd linger, drinking ever so slowly, watching for the dimple that appeared under her left eye whenever she smiled at him. He'd stare at her so long that one of the older boys would have to push him out of the way to get his turn. For as long as he could remember, all Lemuel had ever wanted in life was to one day marry Sally.

By now, Martin Tucker was thirty, still strong and fit, but completely isolated from other people. With no white companionship, he'd finally grown morose and angry and, of course, he could find no comfort in the Scriptures or by keeping a journal. Gradually his anger had hardened into meanness, which he'd begun to take out on the hapless slaves under his control.

By the time Sally was sold, she had grown into a beautiful dark-skinned girl with a flawless face and an unforgettable body. As soon as Tucker laid eyes on her, as she stood with the other nine newly arrived workers, he recognized the solution to his loneliness.

Tucker circled the group once, then stopped right in front of Sally. "You! Gal! Get over here!" He grabbed her arm and walked her some distance away from the others, careful to remain facing them so he could keep watch over them the whole time he was speaking to her. "What they call you, gal?"

"Sally, Masta."

"Well, you sure a pretty lil thing, Sally. I think I'm a take you t' my house. You'll like that won't cha? 'Course you would." He wasn't really asking a question nor did he expect an answer.

Terrified, Sally looked all around for help. For that single moment, all she wanted was to break free from this man's grip. But then the danger in her situation struck home. If this overseer wanted her, what would he do if he suspected that she loved another slave in the group? She could sense Lemuel's agony even though he was behind her with the others. She silently prayed that he wouldn't move or speak.

Indeed, it took all of his strength for Lemuel to keep still. When their former owner had assembled the ten men and women he'd just sold, he'd assured them that their new owner was a wealthy man who would be able to take good care of them. Lemuel had neither believed nor disbelieved; all that had mattered to him was that Sally would be with him. Now this white man was claiming her and there was nothing at all he could do!

Back at their former home, the overseer had taken one of the young women to live with him. She already had a husband and a new baby, but that had made no difference to the overseer; the poor husband had to give her up and get another woman, one who had also just given birth, to wet-nurse his infant. Once the woman became the overseer's mistress, she was forbidden even to speak to any of the other slaves. People hardly ever saw her, except when she'd come outside to wash and hang up her master's clothes.

Lemuel just knew this would be Sally's fate too. He fought a rising tide of anguish as the overseer, whose name he didn't yet know, strode off dragging Sally behind him

Tucker shouted orders over his shoulder to the leader of several slaves who had gathered nearby to see the newcomers. "You! Peter! Take them new niggers down t' the south field an set 'em t' work clearin' some a them tree stumps! An as fer the rest of you, the whole lot a you lazy devils better be workin' time I get back!" Then he pulled Sally up a short dirt path leading to his small log cabin, opened the door, pushed her inside, and followed, slamming the door shut behind him.

Peter approached the stunned group, gesturing for them to follow him. "Better you come on 'long quick now. Masta Tucker, he real mean if'n folks don't obey right smart."

The group followed Peter, with Lemuel bringing up the rear. He stole furtive glances back at the cabin as they made their way across a clearing. But all too soon, they entered a thicket that cut off his view. To Lemuel, it felt as though he had been thrust into Hell. He was sure Sally was lost to him forever!

Inside his cabin, Martin Tucker surveyed his acquisition. Black as she was, the girl was still truly lovely. Tucker circled her once, then again. Sally was trembling visibly and he guessed at the reason. "You ain't never been with a man before, have you?"

"N-n-no, Masta." Large tears had gathered in both eyes and were now making their way down her cheeks.

"Well, you gone learn how good it feels t' have a *real* man teach you." Tucker was grinning as he spoke, believing he was putting her at ease. After all, he reasoned, being chosen as his mistress was more than any nigger girl could possibly hope for. "You just dry up them tears now."

Try as she might, Sally could not stop crying. Terror and revulsion were knotting her stomach so that she could feel her insides roiling. Everything in the room began to spin slowly and she reached out with both hands, trying to steady herself and to stop the sickening motion. The spinning was the last thing she remembered before the world went completely black.

Tucker watched in amazement as the girl crumpled at his feet. "'Cain't believe she that scairt of me," he told himself. He knelt and patted her face. When that produced no response, he scooped her up and laid her on his narrow bed. Then he went outside to fetch water from the rain barrel by the door, grabbing the dipper that hung on an iron nail just above the barrel. He filled the dipper half-way then returned to the bed. Sally still hadn't regained consciousness.

Before attempting to raise the girl's head, Tucker hesitated. For several moments, he stood there gazing at her face. Softly rounded cheeks served as pillows for thick eyelashes; her small upturned nose rose above two gloriously full, perfectly-formed lips that were just slightly parted. He could feel a powerful stirring inside him, the beginnings of some terrible storm threatening to overwhelm his heart. He couldn't put a name to it, this thing, this awful sensation, but it frightened him, and he had only one reaction to fear. He flung the contents of the dipper in Sally's face and shouted, "Wake up, gal!!"

The sudden splash of water woke her immediately; Sally sat up and looked around wildly, her eyes finally locking with Tucker's. Silently, they stared at one another as the air in the cramped cabin became still and thick. Flies buzzed audibly as they bumped against the single tar-papered window, trying to find a way out.

"I ain't got no more time just now," Tucker's gruff voice broke the silence, "I'm a have to take care a you later. Git yerself cleaned up an wait here 'til I get back. Don't cha go nowhere now. You hear?"

He turned and headed for the door, then stopped. As scared as she obviously was, he knew she couldn't be trusted not to run. The walls and floor of the cabin were littered with implements of captivity: hobbles, irons, ropes and lengths of chain. He selected a small leather hobble, the kind used to limit the movement of a calf or colt. Sally was still on his bed, where she'd drawn her legs up and wrapped both arms around them as if trying to make herself as small as possible. Tucker approached the bed, grabbed both her ankles and bound them with the hobble's double leather strap, drawing the open end over and under a metal ring in the back then knotting it around a short chain attached to the ring. Now, she could get up and move around, but only at a shuffle. He was pretty certain that she wouldn't be able to unfasten his knots, even if she did nothing else for the rest of the day but try to get free. "Do like I told you, now," he said, and then he was gone.

Sally knew she was going to be sick. At the same time, she realized how dangerous it would be to soil herself and this white

man's floor, no matter how dirty it was. Swinging her feet over
the side of Tucker's bed, she tested the hobble's limits and found
that she could move about by carefully shifting her weight from
one foot to the other in a side-to-side forward waddle. She was
just able to get to the door, open it, and shuffle/hop to the nearest
tree. There she pulled her skirt up around her waist, squatted and
disgorged everything she'd eaten for the last two days, vomiting
and defecating at the same time.

After a terrifying eternity, the torrent finally ended. Stiffly,
Sally got herself upright and, still holding her skirt waist-high,
started looking all around for some water to clean herself. Her eye
fell on the rain barrel and once again, she shuffled and hopped to
a spot where she could reach into the barrel with one hand while
still holding up her clothing with the other; she could not afford
to soil her only skirt. Fortunately, the barrel was full to the brim
and she was able to scoop up handfuls of water and wash out her
mouth.

Cleaning her bottom was going to be more of a problem, but
she carefully pulled the skirt up over her head, wearing it like a
hood. This freed both hands so she could pull leaves off a nearby
bush to wipe herself. Then it was back to the barrel for more water to wash off whatever remained.

Not far from the front door, there was a narrow bench, just
a split-log resting on a pair of sawhorses. Sally shuffled over to it
and sat. She couldn't bring herself to go back inside that cabin,
but she was afraid to disobey the overseer by trying to go anywhere else.

So, to comfort herself and help pass the time, Sally thought
about Lemuel. In her mind's eye, she could visualize him walking
toward her, smiling widely at her as he always did whenever he
saw her. Lemuel wasn't really handsome, but that smile lit up his
face. And to Sally, that face was the most beautiful thing in her

world. Whatever else happened, she knew she'd have to find some way to see him again.

Just as the sun dipped below the horizon, Martin Tucker was making his way up the dirt road toward his cabin. In the gathering darkness, he could make out the figure seated on his bench. He approached Sally, grinning in anticipation of the pleasures soon to be his. "Glad t'see yer up an about. Look like yer feelin' some better, ain't cha now. C'mon, we goin' inside. I'm a make a woman outa you."

He took hold of one arm while he was speaking and hauled her to her feet. Then he bent down, placed his left shoulder against her waist, hoisting her like a bundle of hay and, pushing the door open, he carried her into the cabin. He kicked the door shut behind him, then unceremoniously tossed her onto his bed and expertly released the hobble.

Sally sat up just as Tucker was unlacing his boots. He sat down heavily beside her on the narrow bed and took them off, followed by his pair of thick woolen stockings. Then he stood and undid the waistband of his rough linen trousers. Once he'd taken them off, he turned to her, clad only in his long shirt. "Well, gal, what'cha waitin' fer?," he laughed. "Get outta them clothes!"

She didn't move. In fact, she seemed to have frozen in place, her legs straight out in front of her, with both hands clutching hard at the fabric of her skirt and her eyes squeezed shut.

"Aw, gal! C'mon now! I ain't gone hurt'cha none!" Tucker shouted, thoroughly exasperated. "Why you takin' on so? You had t'know this was gone happen sometime! Dammit, yer grown!"

Even though he was completely out of patience, something prevented him from simply tearing the garments off her. She was too damnably lovely! "Sally," he spoke more softly, "Listen. You don't have t' take nothin' off. Just lay back n' lemme show you."

Sally realized that she would have to do as he said. She let herself fall backward, eyes still tightly closed, her palms opened in surrender. This was supposed to have been her gift to Lemuel! She held her breath as Tucker's hands groped under her skirt, first freeing her ankles, then moving the fabric up and around her legs. When he'd gotten her skirt up above her thighs and then began nudging them apart, she started crying again.

This time Tucker was too excited to stop, even if he had wanted to. It had just been too long since he'd had a woman. He had always been limited to the female slaves on the farm, and, even then, he'd had to be careful in choosing one. If the woman already had a mate, taking her invariably made her man resentful and obstinate, and thus absolutely worthless as a worker. And the unattached women were little better! The chosen ones would put on airs around their fellow workers and then they'd expect favors from him. Indeed, the last time he'd taken a woman into his cabin, it had nearly caused an insurrection! He'd had to put her out and whip several others, male and female, before things finally quieted down again. But with Sally, Tucker believed he was starting afresh; none of his workers knew these new slaves. She was also quite young, still a virgin, so he could train her to his own satisfaction. And as far as he knew, she was unattached.

As he was about to penetrate her, he suddenly experienced that novel sensation again, like a storm gathering in his chest. And this time it invaded his heart, sending it into a thundering gallop. He plunged into Sally, thrusting and thrusting until he felt the explosion that signaled his climax. Then he rolled off her and lay on his back, gasping, his heart still racing. *This* was completely unexpected! Never had he felt such sweet release!

Sally was entirely unprepared for the pain that seemed to rip her open and paralyze her in the same instant. She wanted to scream, but her mother had warned her, with startling ferocity, not to do so—*ever*.

So instead, Sally focused all her energies on conjuring up her mother, Polly. There she was pulling a too-big linsey-woolsey shift over Sally's head as the child stood, still sleepy, in the darkness of the early morning. She could see Polly, setting about getting her daughter ready for the day, taking up handfuls of Sally's hair, pulling the thick springy tufts through her fingers till the kinky tangles were finally undone, and then, with deft underhand movements, creating two corn-rowed plaits from front to back with a precisely straight center part. Polly would knot together the two stiffly pointy ends of the corn-rows and tuck them into a tiny bun at the nape of Sally's neck. Polly's plaits were so tight that Sally's hair stayed neat for an entire week. A good thing too, since Sally wasn't above sneaking away with Lemuel on warm summer afternoons for a secret swim in the nearby creek.

Sally could hear her mother's voice, scolding her about running off, calling her "lazy" and "willful." Polly scolded so much that sometimes it seemed to Sally that her mother didn't love her at all. And yet, somehow, that thought didn't bother her really. Polly's harsh words and occasional slaps were no different from how the other slaves' children were treated. It was just the way things were.

And Polly had told her, "When a man do what he gone do t' you one day, you best not holler! Else he hurt you worse!"

Polly would never explain to her daughter exactly what a man was "gone do" to her, and when Sally had tried to ask, she'd gotten soundly slapped, as usual, for talking out of turn.

It wasn't that Polly had wanted to hurt her daughter; it was actually that she had been watching the girl grow into a real beauty.

And that meant Sally would, all too soon, come to the attention of any man with eyes in his head. Polly knew how Sally and Lemuel had always felt about each other, but she knew it would make no difference if the man who wanted her daughter was white. And Polly couldn't bring herself to say any of those words out loud to her daughter. It was less painful just to give the girl a simple warning and otherwise keep her in ignorance.

And now, in this awful moment, Sally finally understood her mother's simple warning; she bit her lower lip until she could taste her own blood, waiting in agony for the overseer to finish. She could feel a warm wetness spreading under her hips, but she had no idea it meant she was bleeding. When he finally got off of her, she carefully slid both hands down the front of her body to the damp spot. Shifting ever so slightly so as not to attract the man's attention, she was able to raise her skirt enough to avoid soiling it with her blood.

Tucker turned then and, resting on one elbow, reached out and very gently stroked Sally's cheek. Her eyes were closed; perhaps she'd drifted off. He could feel sleep closing in on him too, as he gathered her against him, wrapping one arm around her waist and cradling her head with the other.

Sally was far from asleep. Every sense in her was wide awake and still screaming with pain. But she forced herself to stay perfectly still as she listened to Tucker's steady breathing. Eventually he began to snore, at which point she carefully eased herself out of his embrace.

There was barely room enough on the bed for one person; when Tucker shifted into his likely accustomed position, flat on his back and dead-center, Sally found herself pushed to the edge, with one foot on the floor. She got up, found her way to the door and went outside to wash her bottom once again. When she felt almost clean enough, she slipped back inside the cabin and, feeling around in the dark, found a chair. There she sat for the rest of the night watching the figure on the bed. Tucker didn't move once through the entire night.

Gradually, the night's blackness faded to a pale grey as light began to filter in through the tiny window. Sally got up from her seat and, as quietly as she could, got onto the bed, her back to Tucker. Almost immediately, he turned on his side, reached over and pulled her in close, wrapping one of his legs around both of hers.

Tucker awakened to full daylight. Realizing he'd overslept, he leapt out of bed and, grabbing stockings and trousers, quickly dressed. As he was pulling on his shoes, he called out sharply, "Sally! Gal! We done slept too long! Get up an fetch some water. You know how t' cook, gal?"

"Yessir, Masta." Sally got up immediately. Since she had spent the night in her clothes, she needed no getting ready. "What must I cook?"

"Ain't got time t' show you." He was lacing up the shoes as he spoke. "Just look around an cook up whatever you find. I'll be back later t' eat." The door closed behind him.

She opened every cupboard and looked in every corner of the cabin. Eventually she came across a sack of cornmeal, several ears of corn and a small side of bacon. This was the kind of food slaves ate. So the overseer dined no better than his workers! Worse yet, he had only three cooking utensils—a kettle, an iron pot, and a skillet.

Remembering that she'd used water from the rain barrel to wash herself, Sally went to find a fresh source. She located the well behind the cabin under a stone slab, and a wooden bucket on a long rope sat nearby. She moved the heavy slab aside and lowered the bucket, then pulled it back up. The well water was fresh and cold. Sally took a long drink before hauling the overflowing bucket back to the cabin.

She set to work boiling corn in the kettle, mixing the corn-meal and water together in the pot to make mush. She found a sharp knife, sliced up the bacon and fried it in the skillet. Once the food was ready, she left everything on the hearth and went back outside to the bench. There was no way that she could eat anything. In fact, Sally wasn't certain she'd ever be able to even look at food again.

CHAPTER 3

*I*t had been three days since Sally had been taken from him, and Lemuel was completely at his wit's end. Part of him wanted to die. What use would his life be if he could never see her again? But a deeper part, buried in the depths of his heart, *knew* with absolute certainty that she needed him to stay alive. And so he chose to go through the motions. Rising with the other slaves before dawn, he would make his way into the fields and spend the days dislodging the stumps of ancient trees in a field destined to grow corn and rye.

The slaves on this farm were housed in separate shanties, some with several families apiece, depending on the size of the family. Lemuel and the other unattached men shared a single shack that had only a door, with no windows and no fireplace. These men had to eat with whichever families were willing to cook up their rations. Fortunately, cooperation was the rule rather than the exception and the women, though equally tired from their days in the fields, were all more than willing to share in cooking for the single men. Thus each family "took in" one man, adding his food ration to the family's pot.

An older woman named Mary had approached Lemuel at the end of the first day. He'd been standing apart from the other workers, so lost he scarcely seemed to know where he was. "Son, if'n you hopes t' eat tonight, you best come on along with me," she'd told him gently. Taking his arm, she'd led him to the shanty where she lived with her husband, Zack and their six children. Rations were given out once a month and none had been provided for the ten new slaves. Nevertheless, Mary cheerfully stretched the family's meal of corn mush and dandelion greens, doling out smaller portions so there was enough for Lemuel too.

Mary was actually only thirty-five but appeared much older, the result of too many years spent in hard work outdoors. Zack had been crippled years before when he'd fallen under a wagon clearing rocks from a new field. One of the wheels had rolled over both his legs, crushing them just below the knees. Unable to walk, he'd learned how to haul himself about using his strong arms and powerful back. Now he minded all the other workers' small children while their parents were at work in the fields.

Lemuel could see that there wasn't enough food and he couldn't muster any kind of an appetite. So, when Mary wasn't looking, he gave his portion to the eldest child, a lad his age named Luke. "You an the other chil'ren take an eat this. I cain't git nothin' down," he whispered.

Luke was ravenous, having put in a long day with nothing but water since early that morning. He ate most of what Lemuel had given him before doling out what was left to his five brothers and sisters.

Zack watched the exchange without commenting. After the meal was done, he swung his body over to the hearth where Lemuel was sitting and staring into the fire. "Son," he said softly, "I reckon you done what you thought was right, seein' as how you's all broke up 'bout somethin'. But you gone need all a yer strength. This here some hard work Masta Tucker gone throw on you. Whatever layin' on yer heart, don't let take yer food."

Those kind, gentle words somehow burst the dam of grief that Lemuel had been holding back with all his might. He collapsed against the fireplace wall, tears coming hard and fast. "It's Sally," he sobbed. "The ovaseer taken my Sally! I ain't never gone see her no more!"

Mary came over to sit beside Lemuel and when he'd started to cry, she put her arms around him and embraced him. Weeping uncontrollably, he buried his face in her shoulder. Over his head, she and her husband shared worried looks. The lad was quite correct; his girl was lost to him forever, or at least for as long as Master Tucker still wanted her.

On the third night, long after he'd left supper at Mary and Zack's shanty, Lemuel lay on his blanket among the other snoring men. Eyes closed, he let his mind wander toward the overseer's cabin–and to Sally.

A small sound outside the single men's shack brought him upright and Lemuel quietly got to his feet. He cracked the door, just enough to put his head out. And there stood Sally, not two feet from the door.

Lemuel would later swear to himself that his heart had stopped dead at the sight of her and that was the reason he hadn't run to her instantly.

"Lemuel," she whispered, gesturing quickly for him to come out.

"Lemuel," she said again, "It's me! It's yer Sally!"

Her voice! He knew that he was just dreaming but, in his heart, Lemuel flew to Sally, catching her up in a near crushing embrace. He kissed her long and hard, finally tasting the amazing sweetness that, up until now, he'd only been able to imagine.

"We ain't got much time, but I just had to see you!" Sally's breathless voice came amidst kisses covering his face and neck. She pulled him into a thicket behind the shack and began to undo his trousers.

For just a moment, as he watched her quickly removing her skirt,

Lemuel wondered when Sally had become so forward. But then he remembered who she'd been with. Lemuel knew she was no longer a virgin, but that couldn't matter, not now! She was still, and would always be his Sally; her being here tonight proved it!

Lemuel let her take the lead, since he'd never actually made love before. Sally had him lie down as she straddled him, guiding him into her most secret place. Her touch set every inch of his body on fire and their climax was one glorious eruption, followed by shuddering gasps.

It was over all too soon. Sally got up first, stepped into her skirt and pulled it up, tying its drawstring tightly around her waist. Lemuel struggled to his feet, still thoroughly shaken. Sally gave him a quick embrace and a kiss. He caught her and held her fast.

"Lemuel, I got to git back 'for Masta Tucker wake up."

"Oh, Sally! I donno if'n I can stand thinkin' about him touchin' you like I just done."

"He ain't never gone be able t' touch me like you. He ain't never gone make me feel like you do. I loves you. I ain't never gone love him!" With that, she was gone.

Lemuel felt himself being shaken roughly awake. "Nigger!" the voice growled in his ear. "Ain't cha heard the horn?" The man whose blanket was next to his had been trying to wake him in vain for several minutes. Rubbing the sleep out of his eyes, Lemuel struggled to his feet and rolled up his blanket. As he joined the other men outside the shack, he couldn't help smiling. Even if it was just a dream, his heart told him that Sally still loved him.

CHAPTER 4

a week after Lemuel's dream, a team of horses drawing a heavily laden wagon appeared on the road leading to the farm. It was the regular monthly delivery of supplies from Albany, the arrangement originally set up by the late Reverend Van Driessen and continued by his son.Once the teamsters, two white men, had unloaded their wagon and Tucker had ordered his workers to "git them provisions in storage!" they would usually stop by Tucker's cabin while the wagon was being reloaded with the farm's produce. To pass the time, they'd sit long enough to share a drink and some local news before continuing on to the next farm on their route. This visit was no different except that the two men seemingly couldn't keep their eyes off Sally.

"Gotcha a new one, ay? She's a tasty bit, that she is!"

"Blacker'n I likes them though."

Tucker poured two fingers of corn mash into each man's tankard, then considerably more into his own. "She ain't yorn t' like now, is she?" he said, downing his drink in a single swallow. "Black or not, lemme show you how yer suppose t' treat yer woman. Sally! Git these gentlemen some more a' that likker from out back! An don't move slow like you usually does."

By now, Sally and Tucker had settled into an elaborate dance of mutual deception. He believed he'd finally found the perfect mistress; Sally fully satisfied him sexually and that should have been enough. But what still disturbed him was how much she also excited his heart and even his soul. And, whenever the dreaded emotions would well up inside him, he'd become irritated. When he was not making love to her, he spent most of their time together, loudly accusing her of stupidity or carelessness. Sally, for her part, played her role as well. She had finally managed to completely mask her loathing of everything about him. If Tucker shouted at her to fetch something, she quickly obeyed, just as she did now, hurrying out and returning with a full jug, almost before he'd finished demanding it. The teamsters drank another round, eyed her up and down, and then were on their way.

Every other month, Petrus Van Driessen's accountant also would visit the farm, usually driving his own buggy and arriving just ahead of the delivery wagon. His name was Jason Firth, and Mr. Firth to the overseer. Tucker had never learned the accountant's first name because of the vast social gulf between them. Mr. Firth would take stock of changes in the number of slaves as a result of births and deaths, how much land was under cultivation, and the yield per acre. The amount and nature of the supplies provided to the farm depended upon the accuracy of this information.

Tucker had devised an accounting system of his own that allowed him to keep on top of such things. On one wall in his cabin, he'd made a series of crude charcoal drawings, much like his own form of hieroglyphics, using tiny stick figures representing slaves and livestock, and little bundles for produce. He would record changes by adding or erasing the correct number of drawings. Tucker was quite proud of his system, so much so that he'd happily shown it to Mr. Firth as soon as it was perfected.

In fact, Mr. Firth thought that both Tucker and his "system" were ignorant, but useful. The accountant would draw up a chair and table facing that wall, then translate Tucker's drawings into numbers recorded in his ledgers. Then, without needing to engage in more than perfunctory conversation, he'd take his leave, usually in enough time to be back in Albany before nightfall.

Shortly after the delivery of supplies and a month before the next visit by the accountant, Sally began to notice changes in her body. Suddenly her skirt no longer fit in the waist and the bodice of her blouse was too tight. She had no idea that she'd been eating so much; it seemed like she'd just barely gotten her appetite back.

It was Tucker who told her what was happening to her. He said, "Gal, you got my bun in yer oven! Didn't ya even suspect it? Ain't cha missed yer bleedin'?"

Sally was horrified. Her periods had only begun the previous year and had been irregular from the first; in fact, she hadn't had one since coming to the Van Driessen farm.

"Masta, wha-what's a 'bun-in-th'-oven'?"

Tucker was about to laugh at her, but the look on her face stopped him. Her eyes had grown so wide and were filling with tears, and her lower lip was trembling. Suddenly, he wanted to grab her up in his arms and kiss away each of her tears. The surging in his chest was almost unbearable.

Instead, he answered her gruffly, "Don't be so stupid! Means yer gone have a baby's what it means. I keep tellin' ya t' grow up!" A moment later, he added, "Listen, Sally, it ain't so bad. I'm a get one a' the womens what knows about such things t' take care a' ya. An' next month, I'm a get' cha a extra bolt a' cloth fer ya t' make ya some dresses what'll fit' cha."

CHAPTER 5

*I*t wasn't just the pregnancy that sent Sally into the depths of despair. How could she expect Lemuel to still love her with this happening to her? Even though Tucker had confined her to his cabin and the immediate grounds around it, she'd been plotting from that first night how to find Lemuel and let him know she was still his, at least in her heart. Now she also would have to tell him she was expecting Tucker's child. Yet it never crossed her mind to keep it from him; she'd always told Lemuel the truth.

One thing Sally had noticed from the first about Tucker was that the man slept like the dead; nothing seemed to rouse him. She had stayed awake watching him night after night, and had tested trying to wake him by moving the chairs and tables around. She'd even slammed the cabin door a few times. She kept this up until she was certain that he wouldn't notice her absence from his bed.

On the same night that she realized she was pregnant, Sally slipped out of the cabin for the first time as soon as she was sure Tucker was sound asleep. She'd had no idea where the slaves' quarters were, but knew she needed to explore as much of the grounds as she could cover in the few hours before first light.

Right behind Tucker's cabin was an ancient forest whose massive evergreens had never known an axe. Growing in the shadow of these giants were low-slung woodlands of pines and myrtle bushes. This entire forest remained in deep shadow, even on the brightest of days, and at night, the gloom was completely im-penetrable. Sally was determined to find out where Lemuel slept. Once she did, in order to get there without attracting anyone's notice, she'd need a route that completely bypassed the farm's main road. Although its darkness had frightened her from the first days at Tucker's cabin, Sally decided to try exploring this for-est, both in daylight and at night, just to see if it could provide her with a safe route.

She chose mornings, not long after Tucker had left, to walk the forest's perimeter. Keeping the sun on her right, she followed the tree line north for as long as she could go until the sun had moved directly overhead. Then she turned and headed back the way she'd come. Obviously, the virgin forest stretched northward for many more miles. Back at the cabin she did the same thing, but this time headed south. Here, the trees were more widely spaced and inter-spersed with old stumps, showing that many had been felled, most likely for lumber. This was probably the part of the forest clos-est to the rest of the farm. Sally knew she could spend no more than about an hour each day in her explorations, and then only on sunny days so she could keep track of the time. But despite these limitations, she was able to learn much about her potential route.

The baby was born six months later—a tiny girl, coffee-and-cream colored, with curly black hair. Mary had been the one to attend the birth of Sally's child; there was no proper midwife on the farm, but Mary, having borne six children, all alive, had the most experience. Tucker had been out in the field supervising the planting of a newly cleared field when Mary sent word that his first child had been born. He left Peter in charge and hurried back to the cabin.

Sally was trying to nurse the infant under Mary's direction. When Tucker arrived, he barely glanced at the baby; he picked up a piece of charcoal and drew a tiny figure on his wall. Then he told Mary to go outside and "stay 'til yer called fer."

"Sally," he began, "Something you got t' understand. This baby ain't yorn. T'ain't mine neither. She belongs t' the man what owns this farm. So, I cain't let'cha git too attached. I'm'a allow you t' nurse her 'til she can eat solid. Then I got t' send her t' live with the others. I'm tellin' ya now so's you can git use 't the idea."

Sally had been staring avidly at this amazing bundle ever since Mary had handed the baby to her. The infant, so light in her arms, pushed her tiny limbs against the thin blanket that Mary had wrapped tightly around her. Sally was so enraptured she couldn't really fix on what Tucker was saying; in fact, she didn't even look up.

"Gal! Ain'cha heard me? I said it ain't yorn! Now I'm a git that woman back in here t' clean ya up." Tucker headed for the open door as he was speaking. "Mary!" he shouted, although he needn't have, since she was right there. "Git back in here! You can stay with Sally 'till I git back t' night. Make shore she don't hold that baby fer too long!"

Once the door had closed behind the overseer, Mary gently took the infant and laid her in the small wooden box she had brought from her shack. It had served as a cradle for each of her own children. She then stood by the bed, silently studying Sally. So, this was the girl that poor Lemuel, was grieving over so badly. Sally had weathered her first labor surprisingly well, considering how young she was. She'd cried out only once or twice, and the delivery had actually been quite easy. This girl was a born breeder; Tucker was probably going to keep her pregnant. Mary shook her head sadly.

"Chile," the older woman began softly, "You need t' mind what Masta Tucker sayin' about'cha chil'ren. You cain't let none a' em git too close. It'll hurt'cha heart too bad when ya got t' turn 'em loose."

For the first time Sally heard those all-important words. "What'cha mean I got t' turn m'own chile loose? Why I got t' do that? I had her! She mine! That my chile!" Sally was shouting by now; an almost blinding anger seizing her. No one, not Tucker nor this woman was going to take her child!

"I knows how you feel, chile, but ain't none 'a our chil'ren belongs t' us. Even Masta Tucker ain't got no say about that. He don't own us; he just the ovaseer. Listen," Mary went on, "Lemme tell you what I'm talkin' 'bout."

She drew Master Tucker's chair close to the bed and sat, eyes closed for a full minute before continuing. "The nigger what Masta Tucker depends on the most 'round here, he be name Peter. Well, Peter an his wife Lucy, they had three chil'ren: a boy, the oldest, he be name Paul, an two li'l gals be name Peggy an' Jenny. Well, the man what own this farm back then, he wanna git some servants fer his own chil'ren. He send word t' Masta Tucker t' pick out three good young'uns. Seem like servants fer white chil'ren got t' be train up from real young. An them servant chil'ren got t' be quick too 'bout learnin' what they got t' do.

"Everybody 'round here know how good Peter an Lucy three chil'ren was, 'cause Lucy raise 'em up right! She were strict, but she love 'em too. An' Peter, well, the sun rise an set on them chil'ren. Was'nt nothin' he wouldn't do fer 'um, but he back up his wife if'n she had t' lay down the law with one 'r another of 'um."

Mary had started rocking slowly as she spoke; now a distant look came into her eyes.

"Time come t' pick out the chil'ren, Masta Tucker pick out Peter an Lucy young'uns, all three! When Masta Tucker told Peter, seem like the man near 'bout went crazy. He cried an beg Masta not t' take all a his chil'ren. It were just awful the way that man cried–cried just like a babe, what he done. Masta Tucker, he only been ovaseer a few years, so he ain't know what else t' do 'cept t' beat Peter 'til he hush up. After Masta whip him, he told Peter t' just go on an have some more chil'ren. But it weren't that easy. Peter, he weren't that young no more, an Lucy, she older'n him. They tried fer the longest and it look like they wasn't gone never have another 'un. Lord had mercy on 'um though. He give 'um one last child, just 'fore Lucy died."

Here, Mary stopped abruptly, sniffed and quickly wiped her eyes with the back of one hand before continuing.

"What I'm sayin', if'n the man what own this farm take a notion t' sell us off or t' take our chil'ren, ain't nothin nobody can do 'bout it. "An that include Masta Tucker!"

Tears filled Sally's eyes during Mary's tale. Now they ran freely down her cheeks and under her chin, forming large drops that fell onto the bedclothes. Mary lifted the infant and placed her back in Sally's arms. She used a corner of the sheet to wipe Sally's face. "Just enjoy her while you kin. Nurse her an don't worry 'bout what come later. You need t' give her a name though. What'cha wanna call her?"

The question made Sally immediately think of Lemuel. It seemed so long ago now, but she and Lemuel had decided on names for their future children, at least the first boy and girl. Lemuel's father had been called Manuel; that was to be their boy child's name. The first girl would be Polly, after Sally's mother. But this wasn't Lemuel's child.

"I'll call her Mary. Would that be alright?"

"If'n that's what'cha want, I'd be right proud. 'An don't 'cha worry none. Us womens always taken care a each other chil'ren. I'm a raise yourn myself."

Sally gazed down at her newly-named daughter, absently adjusting the blanket. With eyes still lowered she spoke up tentatively. "Miz Mary, you ever see a worker called Lemuel? He come on the place same time I did."

"Why yes, I seen him. He take his meals with me an Zack an our chil'ren every evenin'. Think I know why you askin' too. He were yer beau. Right?" Mary tried her best to hide a slight smile.

"Oh please, do tell me how he doin'! I ain't seem him since Masta Tucker taken me that first day!"

Mary hesitated before answering carefully, "He doin' better now. He were broke up when I first seen him, but I believe he done got use t' the idea. Don't none a' us like being separated from who we loves, but we all got t' get used t' it sometime r' nother."

Sally didn't respond for several minutes while she fiddled with Mary's blankets. When she spoke again, it was to ask, "Do he stay with you?"

"Oh no! He sleep in the single men's shack. Lord! It the worst place in the quarters! Big ole holes all 'long the back wall. Don't nobody got no time t' be fixin' up they houses though, so it just stay that way. Bad thing 'bout it bein' so broke down, it be the last shack in the row. Wind blow hard in winter, ain't no shack on the back side t' help keep out the cold."

Now Sally knew exactly where Lemuel was each night. If she could find the slaves' quarters, she could easily recognize the single men's shack. She wondered whether Mary had intended to supply this much information. But she decided not to let on how much she was taking it all in.

"Miz Mary, 'fore you go, would you show me how t' feed Mary again?"

Another thing about Tucker that Sally observed in the weeks following Mary's birth was that the overseer made it a point to ignore how much time she spent caring for the baby as much as possible. When she nursed Mary in the evenings after he returned to the cabin, he'd always look away. And he never seemed to hear the baby cry at night. In fact, it seemed that he slept more soundly now than ever.

By the time Mary was three months old, she finally slept through the night. Now, Sally realized, was her chance to locate the single men's shack by trying out her pre-planned route through the woods. During the day, Sally had bundled up Mary and, together they had traced a path along the edge of the farm just behind the first line of trees. These large old trees provided complete cover to anyone walking even a few feet within the forest's gloom. Sally had been able to explore enough of the farm to recognize what surely had to be the slaves' quarters and to gauge the distance from Tucker's cabin. After watching her daughter through the night for a week, Sally decided it was safe to leave her sleeping and at last go find Lemuel. She just wanted to see his face and tell him about Mary, although she had no idea how he would react. She could only pray that he wouldn't be too hurt or angry.

The single men's shack was easily recognizable, even from her hidden path. The back wall had been roughly patched, but it showed several open holes. Sally approached one of the holes and tried to peer inside but it was impossible to make out anyone among the forms bundled under blankets on the floor. She moved from one hole to another, then another. At last, she ventured around to the front where there was a door. She pushed tentatively against it, opening it just a little.

She hadn't thought about how to attract Lemuel's attention without waking the other men. Suddenly, she remembered a signal they'd used when they wanted to meet without alerting either of their parents—a low whistle that Lemuel had taught her. Crouching at the door, she whistled once, waited, and then did it again. After the third whistle, someone inside stirred and sat up. Sally rose swiftly and ran back from the door in case she'd awakened someone other than Lemuel.

When he came outside, Sally could see that it was Lemuel. She stepped out of the shadows and made a small gesture with one hand.

"It's me," she said simply

Lemuel walked quickly toward her and then stopped. "Sally?"

"It's me," she repeated.

Lemuel didn't move, but Sally took a step closer. This time, she beckoned to him to follow her. Leading the way, she headed back a short ways into the woods. There, she turned, facing him squarely and took a deep breath.

"Lemuel, I–I done had a baby. I ain't wanna, but I couldn't help it." Sally began to cry. "I name her Mary, 'cause Miz Mary helped me have her. An Masta Tucker say she don't belong t' me nohow! I–I ain't wanna bring this but I just had t' find you!" Sally was crying so hard by now that she could barely speak.

Lemuel caught her up and held her tightly. Sally let herself be held for a moment. Then, she wrapped both arms around his neck and began to kiss his face, cheeks, nose, eyes, and everywhere. She reached for the waistband of his trousers and began to untie the cord.

"Sally, what'cha doin'?" Lemuel moaned. But then he just as quickly began to undo her skirt. Together, they fell to the ground and continued to undress each other.

Fortunately, the night wasn't too chilly and their lovemaking created more than enough heat. When it was over, Lemuel took Sally onto his lap and rocked her like a baby.

"I been dreamin' 'bout'cha comin' like this fer the longest. Ain't think it was really gone happen though," he whispered against her crisp thick hair.

"Can you still love me, even after I had m' babe?"

"More, Sally. More n' ever."

Sally slowly traced his lips with her fingers. She knew she needed to dress and get back to the cabin. No telling how late it was by now. Reluctantly, she got up, slipped her bodice over her head and stepped into her skirt. Lemuel watched her intently.

"You ain't look no different," he said softly. "Like y' ain't had no babe a' tall."

"You different," she answered. "Taller an stronger—an real good-lookin' too! Not that you wasn't always—at least t' me."

"Sally, wait. How you come t' find me?" Lemuel asked, eager to keep her just a few moments longer. "Everybody say Masta Tucker don't never let you nowhere near where the workers be at."

Sally sat back down next to him. He immediately pulled her close—so close that she could take in his so-well remembered scent with each breath.

"Miz Mary let on where the men sleep at when she come t' help me."

"Ain't Masta Tucker like t' wake up an find out you gone?" Lemuel asked, gently stroking her cheek with his free hand. "An what about 'cha babe? What if she cry an wake him up?"

Sally laughed, "That man sleep like he dead! He don't wake up fer nothin'! Not the babe crying, not nothin'! I done spent more nights slammin' doors an draggin' chairs around t' make sure a that. An as fer Mary, she sleepin' through the night, too, now. I made sure a that, too."

"You always was the smart one." Lemuel was laughing now as well. "Member how, when we was little, you was the one always figgered out how t' get us away from our chores so we could play?"

"Yeah," Sally answered. "But you was smart enough so's we never got caught. You could always tell if'n it were safe t' go. An you wouldn't go if'n it weren't."

Lemuel got slowly to his feet, bringing Sally up with him. He hugged her tightly and then released her firmly.

"You git on back now" he said gently. "I don't want nothin' t' happen t' you—even if'n Masta Tucker do sleep like you say. You still brave an smart but…."his voice trailed off.

They stood gazing at each other for the longest moment before Sally finally turned and walked slowly into the shadows. Lemuel watched the gloom swallow her form before returning to the men's shack and slipping inside.

Back at Tucker's cabin, Sally quietly let herself inside. She didn't think Tucker would wake up, but she didn't want Mary to be startled and cry out. Both were sleeping soundly. Sally took off her clothes and hid them under a bundle set aside for washing. Then she climbed onto the narrow bed next to Tucker. For the first time since coming to the farm, she slept soundly.

One evening, when Mary was about eight months old, Sally took her up to nurse. This time, the little girl refused the breast. She squirmed off Sally's lap and toddled around the cabin laughing each time her mother scooped her up and tried again. When Tucker got home that night, Sally still hadn't fed her daughter.

"That li'l gal's ready fer solid food!" he announced with barely suppressed glee. "Tomorrow, want'cha t' take her down t' Mary's cabin. We gone finally git some quiet 'round here!"

"Masta Tucker, she ain't ready yet." Sally's eyes filled. Unconsciously, she clasped her hands pleadingly. "Cain't I keep her just a little longer?"

"Gal! What I told ya 'bout gettin' too attached?" he shouted suddenly. "Do like I told ya!" Then, just as suddenly, he snatched up his hat and stormed out of the cabin, slamming the door behind him.

All through that night, Sally sat up hugging and rocking her daughter. Tucker sat up with them for a while, silently watching, before finally turning in. Surprisingly, he never demanded that she put Mary down and come service him.

Early the next morning, Sally dressed herself and Mary. Then, as she was serving Tucker his coffee and cornbread, she asked him sullenly, "Masta, where I'm 'sposed t' go? I don't know where Mary cabin at. You ain't never let me go near where the workers live."

Without answering her immediately, he finished the bread, drained his cup, opened the door and pointed toward the main road, just down the hill from the cabin door.

"Just follow that road 'til y' git t' a row a broke-down shacks. Mary's the fourth one in. Got a whole bunch a' li'l niggers runnin' 'round out front. Cain't miss it."

The slaves' quarters were just as Tucker had described them, their shabbiness starkly revealed in the daylight. Sally immediately recognized Mary's shack by the number of children playing about in the dirt outside the front door. It was still early enough that Mary hadn't yet left for the fields. She met Sally in the front yard and immediately took little Mary out of her arms.

"Don't make no fuss in front a' the babe." Mary whispered, leaning close to Sally. "Just kiss her an tell her 'bye. She gone fret some, but don't'cha look back."

Sally did as she was told and Mary took the little girl inside. As she was walking away, Sally steeled herself against turning back toward the shack. A few steps later, she heard her daughter's wails and then burst into tears herself. She cried bitterly for the rest of that day and all of the next.

CHAPTER 6

*O*ver the next five years, Tucker put three more "buns" in Sally's oven, another girl and two boys. She nursed and named each one. There was Sarah, then Zack, after Mary's husband, and finally Simon. As each reached the age of eight months, she obediently carried the baby to Mary's cabin, kissed her child goodbye and left with nary a backward glance. This was to be their final separation; Sally forced herself to ignore the child's cries, even as they broke her heart each time.

Between her pregnancies and while she was still nursing, Sally continued to meet Lemuel in the woods behind the workers' shack. Their trysts were especially difficult in winter; the ground was most often snow-covered and they both risked sickness from staying outdoors, even for the few short hours that Sally could get away. Their only salvation was that the bitter cold kept anyone who might see them indoors.

On just such a winter night, right after a heavy snowfall, Sally was bundled with Lemuel under his blanket on an improvised pallet of straw. To keep out the cold, they had kept on as much of their clothing as possible. Sally took Lemuel's face in both her hands so he wouldn't be able to turn away.

"I done had four a' Masta Tucker babies, an now I'm carryin' the fifth. Ain't havin' another'n unless it yourn," she said firmly.

"Sally. You cain't do that! If'n he find out, he kill you!"

"He won't find out! I ain't had all them chil'ren fer nothin'! I knows just how t' work it so's he ain't never gone know who baby I had!"

"How, Sally? How you gone hide a black baby? Ain't none a Masta Tucker chil'ren come out black! I betcha none a' um ever would neither!"

"Ain't gone never let him see it."

Lemuel wanted to talk Sally out of this thing, but she got up too quickly. Hugging herself for warmth, she took off through the trees in the direction of the overseer's cabin, leaving him to gather up the straw pallet, hide it under a corner of the shack and slip back inside. Even after he'd lain down among the other snoring men and covered himself with his blanket, he couldn't stop the shivering in his body. It wasn't just the icy drafts coming through the chinks in the walls; Lemuel shook from sheer terror.

The whole concept of timing her childbirths had come as a revelation to him. He now wished he'd known what was in Sally's mind before they'd ever started making love. For all he knew, the child she was carrying right now could be his. And even if it wasn't, he didn't doubt for one moment that she was determined to work it out so that the *next* baby *would be*. What if she couldn't hide the fact that one of her babies wasn't Master Tucker's? Sally was just stubborn enough to risk death rather than tell him who the father was.

The following morning, Peter blew the horn summoning everyone to assemble. Outside the single men's shack, workers stamped and slapped themselves attempting to warm their already too-cold bodies. No one owned a real coat or even a woolen frock; men and women had to make do by layering on every piece of clothing they had: double pairs of stockings, trousers, shirts, skirts and blouses. The only salvation was that much work could now be done indoors. Hay had to be bundled and stored;

foodstuffs dried or preserved; tools cleaned and sharpened for spring planting; barns and sheds repaired.

That day, Lemuel was part of a detail sent out under Peter's direction to feed the livestock. The men tramped through deep snow toward the nearby fields where cattle lowed miserably, anxious to be fed and led back to the barn. Peter had been at the head of the group, but now he fell back and in step beside Lemuel. The young man glanced over uneasily, but Peter only trudged along silently, his steps matching Lemuel's. When the group reached the herd huddled together in one corner of the field, the men hauled the bales of hay near enough to loosen and spread some out in front of the animals.

Lemuel leaned into his pitchfork, keeping his head down, hoping Peter would eventually move away. But the older man continued to work next to him almost shoulder to shoulder. By now, Lemuel was beginning to experience a sense of panic. He knew that Peter's cabin was the first one on slaves' row, while the single men's shack was all the way at the end, almost in the woods. Still, Peter could have been out late one night and caught a glimpse of Sally, either coming out of the woods or heading back toward Tucker's cabin. Lemuel had not one bit of doubt that Peter would tell on him and Sally. There was just something about the man, a dead look about the eyes, that always sent icy chills through Lemuel's veins.

The cows, having eaten their fill were now jostling to be herded back inside. Peter patted the head of the one in the lead. Immediately she began following him toward the barn and the others fell in behind her. Without turning, he suddenly spoke up, "Lemuel, want'cha t' come on along. Got somethin' t' talk t' you about."

Lemuel's heart jumped and began thumping loudly. He hurried to catch up. "Yessir?"

"Been noticin' how you always by yerself. "Ain't hardly talk t' nobody 'cept 'n Mary 'n Zack. Look like you don't hardly wanna have nuthin' t' do with nobody else."

"It-it jus' seem like that 'cause I-I be kinda slow when it come t' talkin'. M-m'mind jus' don' seem t' work fast enough t' be conversin'." Lemuel's brain was working very quickly now. What Peter had said was absolutely true. He had deliberately tried to remain as unobtrusive as possible. He didn't realize that he'd appeared snobbish. "Truth is, I likes everybody 'round here. Just shy is all."

"Glad t' hear it. 'Cause I'm a'gitcha some good company. M' daughter, Lucy. I name her after her Ma."

Both men had reached the barn by this time. Peter opened the wide doors and shooed the last of the herd inside. He was facing Lemuel squarely as he spoke about his daughter. A strange light blazed behind his eyes, bringing his whole face to life.

"Lucy a good girl. Sweet an good just like her Ma." The light softened into a sheen, filming both eyes, threatening to become tears. "She a woman now, near-'bout sixteen year, I reckon. Been tryin' t' keep count since her Ma passed." Peter stopped abruptly, struggling against a still-fresh pain, took a breath and then continued, "Had my eye on you ever since ya come on the place. Seem like a hard-workin' nigger. Clean an quiet in yer ways. Maybe make a good enough husband fer my Lucy."

Peter's last words fell into a silence that stretched out between the two men. Lemuel could feel a trickle of icy sweat sliding downward between his shoulder blades. He knew he had to say something. But inside his head, words jumbled and collided meaninglessly. The last thing he'd expected was for Peter to offer him his daughter.

"Thought you'd be happy." Peter's expression hadn't changed, but his eyes had hardened.

"I-I were'nt expectin' what'cha just said." Lemuel could hear his heartbeat so clearly that he feared Peter would be able to hear it. The man had put him in an impossible spot. He could think of no way to refuse, especially when it was clear that Peter was offering up to him the dearest thing in his life.

"You ain't happy 'bout it, though. I kin tell. How come y' don't wanna marry my daughter?" Peter's eyes, cold and dead, locked with Lemuel's.

Lying had never come easily for Lemuel. From childhood, he'd always felt better telling the truth, even when doing so earned him a beating. Now, however, he had Sally to protect. Perhaps he could get by with part of the truth.

"Yer right 'bout the happy part. Truth is, I ain't been happy since I got here. Had to part from my gal when I got sold off. Ain't never got over it. Don't look like I ever will."

Peter's expression softened somewhat. "Well. Cain't make you do what'cha don't wanna. You aughta think about it though. Don't make no sense grievin' over what' cha cain't change." He swung around abruptly and walked off.

Lemuel did think about it. For the next full month he examined the thing from every possible angle. If he agreed to marry Lucy, his and Sally's outdoor trysts would have to end. She would finally be safe. On the other hand, he knew his Sally like he knew his own heart. She could no more stop loving him than he could her. Although she would never try to see him again, she would pine something fierce. And he would be deceiving Lucy every time he came to her as her husband. Sooner or later, she would realize that he didn't, that he couldn't, love her. Somehow he had to put off giving Peter an answer, at least until he could figure a way out of this predicament.

CHAPTER 7

*S*ally had actually made the decision to have Lemuel's baby soon after she discovered she was pregnant for the fifth time. What she'd done over the five years with Tucker was to learn her own cycle intimately. Because she had been pregnant and then nursing so often, she'd experienced very few periods. But she'd noticed that her body would begin to change right after she'd weaned a baby. So she was fairly certain that this was when the next pregnancy was beginning. She'd have to make sure that she was with Lemuel, and only Lemuel, at just the right time. Keeping Master Tucker from taking her first was going to be her most difficult challenge.

On the evening that she delivered Tucker's fifth baby, a boy she would name Tom, Sally refused to eat anything and appeared so weak that she couldn't even sit up to nurse the infant.

After the boy was born, Mary went to fetch Tucker. By now, he took the births of his children in stride; he stayed away until someone came to tell him the news and whether it was a boy or girl. Since it was late autumn, the workers were clearing the fields of the last harvest and spreading a mulch of dried hay and corn stalks. Mary found him watching the men from atop a stone wall.

"Masta Tucker, sir, you need to come quick. Sally ain't doin' so well this time. Seem like she ailin' more then usual."

Tucker leapt down and nearly knocked the woman over running past her at full bore. He tore up the path to his cabin, with Mary barely able to keep up. "Sally," he called out, "Whatsa' matter? Gal, you sick?"

Sally stirred feebly, the newborn resting against her side. "Masta, I sure don't feel too good."

By now Mary stood beside the bed. "Masta Tucker, I believe she got the fever. She ain't gone be able to get up fer a few days. If'n you wants, I can take her to my cabin. Me an Zack can take care a her an the babe."

Tucker rubbed his jaw nervously. He didn't want Sally out of his sight but at the same time, he was afraid to leave her alone in his cabin.

"Naw. I want her to stay here. You stay an watch her 'til she git better."

So, Mary brought a pallet from her cabin and placed it on the floor beside the baby's cradle. During the day, she cooked and tended the infant while Sally spent the time in bed. Sally was eating very little, so little, in fact, that all of her strength went into producing milk. When she wasn't nursing, she slept both day and night.

Tucker was nearly beside himself with worry. Sally had never before been sick, neither when she'd been pregnant nor afterward. He gladly accepted Mary's continued presence in his cabin, even though it meant giving up his bed and sleeping on the floor with a blanket. He often thought about taking Mary's pallet, especially when bugs and other tiny critters invaded his sleeping space, but he couldn't bring himself to lie down on a nigger's bed.

A full week went by with Sally getting no better. Then another week passed the same way. When a third week ended and Sally still hadn't gotten out of bed, Tucker was convinced that he might be losing her. On Sunday morning he decided Sally needed a doctor. The supply wagon was due in two weeks; he would send word to Mr. Van Driessen that they urgently needed a physician.

But then Sally began to rally. Over the next week, she'd stay awake a little longer each day and she ate a bit more of Mary's cooking. By the following Saturday, she was at last able to get out of bed. She asked Tucker to let Mary go back to her own cabin.

"An I don't need no doctor neither," she insisted.

Tucker took Sally at her word. By the time the supplies arrived, she seemed completely cured. She immediately got back to cooking, washing and caring for baby Tom.

Everything was back to normal, except for one small thing that, for Tucker, was a very big thing, a very big thing indeed. On the night of the first day that she was up and working, Sally refused Tucker. When he, having waited for over four weeks, reached for her, Sally placed both hands against his chest. Then she moved away from him.

"Gal!" he demanded, "What the hell you doin'?"

"Masta, I cain't do it yet. It still too sore down there!"

"What'cha mean, still too sore? We ain't never waited this long before!" Tucker could barely contain his raging desire. He could feel its heat spreading from his loins into his belly. "Gal," he hissed, "I cain't wait no longer!"

"Ain't gone make y' wait. Just cain't do it down there."

Sally had begun stroking Tucker's chest, very gently, as she spoke. With the same gentle motion, she let one hand slide down his body. Then, with both arms holding him tightly, she began moving in the now-too-familiar fashion, bringing him to the most amazing climax.

"Gal!" Tucker breathed, when he could finally speak, "You done learnt some new tricks, ain't cha, now!"

He cradled her face gently in both palms. God! She was simply amazing! Try as he might, he knew he would never be able to conquer this – yes he had to admit it – this love he had for Sally. She was in his blood right now, pumping through his heart with each beat. His entire body literally ached with love for this woman.

"Yer gone be alright now," she whispered. "Go on to sleep."

As though she had the power to order it, Tucker felt his eyelids grow heavy. A moment later, he was snoring softly.

Sally lost no time. As soon as she was certain Tucker wouldn't awaken again until sunrise, she got up, dressed in two layers of clothing and slipped out of the cabin to meet Lemuel. She took her accustomed shortcut through the woods. Tonight she would give herself only to him.

For the rest of that autumn, and into early winter, Sally made love to Lemuel alone. She managed to keep Tucker sexually satisfied, while inventing an excuse for not allowing him actual penetration. She told him she had developed an awful female "misery."

"Masta, I don't rightly know what it is," she explained, "but it stink somethin' terrible. An' I be scratchin' down there 'cause it itch so bad!"

Sally discovered that clabber, when smeared on her genitals in the morning, produced by nightfall an odor offensive enough to convince Tucker not to try anything until her problem cleared up. Mary had taught her how to make clabber by setting fresh milk outside until it began to thicken and turn. The sour milk that resulted made excellent biscuits and corn cakes. Sally decided to use this ruse until she was definitely pregnant again – and this time by Lemuel.

Baby Tom had been born at the end of the summer planting season. By mid-winter, he was sitting up almost steadily and trying to move around whenever Sally placed him on a blanket on the floor. In another two months he'd be ready to eat porridge from a spoon. It always saddened Sally when she knew the time for parting with her baby was at hand.

Tucker realized this too. But this time he had a wonderful surprise for Sally. She had gone through an especially difficult winter, what with the earlier illness and her current "female problem." On a snowy evening in early February, he finally revealed his secret.

"Sally, gal, I knowd how much it pained you t' give up yer chil'ren like you done. After this 'un here, y' ain't gone have t' give up no more."

Sally had been stroking Tom's little back as he lay on his stomach, his arms and legs waving vigorously in baby circles. Something in Tucker's voice warned her not to speak yet and to keep her eyes on her child.

"I been saving all a m' pay fer the last five years. Think I got enough put by t' make a offer fer you." Tucker waited for her to say something. When she didn't, he continued. "A breeding nigger woman's worth 'bout £500. But that's if'n she working the fields. All I had you doing was cookin' an cleanin' fer me." He grinned suddenly, "An takin' care a m' other needs. Figger I can git Mr. Firth t' strike a deal fer 'bout £300."

He paused again. Sally remained silent, but this time he wasn't really paying her any attention; he began speaking mostly to the air in front of him. "Soon as I finish off payin fer you, I'm a start in t' savin fer the first rent on a little parcel a land. Figger I kin tenant farm, an you an me an our kids kin work it till I kin git somethin of my own. That way, I won't have t' be a rich man's ovaseer fer the rest a my life."

Tucker had been sitting in his chair beside the fireplace, smoking his Dutch pipe. Sally was on the floor, sharing the blanket with her baby. Slowly, she raised her eyes to meet Tucker's.

"What all that mean, Masta? What'cha talkin' 'bout?"

"It mean I'm a buy you, gal!"

She allowed herself to stare at him blankly.

"An, once I do, yer chil'ren 'll be mine – ourn! Won't nobody be able t' take 'um!" Tucker's eyes clouded over briefly; a memory, painful, insistent, of Peter on his knees begging for his children, passed behind them. He got up abruptly and knocked the ashes out of the pipe. "Now you put that baby t' sleep an come on t' bed. Want'cha t' show me how grateful y' are."

Something in the overseer's voice told Sally that she would have to put on the performance of her life. Clearly, Tucker believed he was giving her a great gift, for which she was supposed be relieved and joyful. Instead, all she could feel was a tightening in the pit of her stomach and an icy finger of fear on the back of her neck. She couldn't let Tucker sense this, so she smiled suddenly – a forced, too-wide grimace.

"Oh Masta! You gone do that? Buy me so I can keep my chil'ren?"

Tucker didn't seem to notice anything false in either her expression or words. He grinned back, showing broken teeth stained brown from tobacco. The overseer's face was not enhanced by his smile. In fact, he looked much better without it. Sally shivered at the sight, glad that the man rarely smiled.

"Masta, I'm a do my best fer you. Sorry I cain't do no more."

After that night, Sally realized she would only be able to keep Tucker satisfied without actual intercourse for a short time longer. So, she made the difficult decision to wean little Tom early. On the very next morning, she used some of her milk to make a thin gruel of finely ground cornmeal. When she tried feeding him the mixture from a spoon, the baby promptly spit it out. Sally tried again, with the same results. By early afternoon, however, Tom was too hungry to resist opening his little mouth when she pressed the hated metal thing against his lips. He finished the entire bowl, and then fell asleep almost immediately.

The novel taste and hunger finally drove her baby to accept this new method of eating. Gradually, Sally reduced the amount of milk in the gruel, replacing it with well water. Tom seemed to tolerate the change well enough, although he still wanted to cuddle at her breast before going to sleep each night. By the end of February, Sally's milk had dried up. By mid-March, she could feel the signs of a new pregnancy.

CHAPTER 8

*F*or the next month, Lemuel avoided being alone. He began working alongside the other men and women, and
socializing with them at night after the day's work was done. He
still took supper with Mary and Zack and their children but he
made it his business to hurry straight from their cabin to the
single men's shack directly afterwards. He knew that Peter wanted
to speak with him again about Lucy, and he knew nothing had
changed.

Peter, for his part, didn't try to approach Lemuel again. In
fact, it began to seem as though he'd forgotten about their conversation. Peter hadn't been in the habit of joining the other workers
in their relaxation anyway. Usually, after blowing the horn for
quitting time, he'd join his daughter and together, they'd make
their way back to his cabin. Lucy would put together a supper for
both of them, then clean up their dishes and take up her mending. There were always pants and shirts that needed patching,
and once a week, she'd spend part of her night outdoors washing
and hanging their clothes. Peter would watch his daughter as she
went about her woman's chores, then he'd take a walk and have a
smoke before bed.

Peter usually liked to wander the perimeter of the farm while
he smoked. But on one of his nocturnal strolls, he'd spied a figure moving between the cabins and the deep woods surrounding

the farm. Something told him to step into the shadows behind a cabin and watch.

Well, I swan, he thought, *if'n it ain't the ovaseer woman! What she doin' out this time of night?*

Keeping to the shadows, Peter followed the figure until she reached the single men's shack. When he saw Lemuel emerge, he suddenly had all the information he needed. This was the true reason for the young man's reticence about courting his daughter.

Peter began making sure his walks included a turn near the woods behind the single men's shack. He was careful to remain at enough of a distance to be hidden in the dark, especially to a couple so clearly intent only upon each other. By the time winter had set in, Peter no longer needed to spy on the lovers. He just needed to decide what to do about them.

He'd mentally chosen Lemuel for Lucy well before he learned the young man's secret. Now he realized that, by having this affair, Sally was risking both her and Lemuel's lives. The girl was completely irresponsible! But a woman as pretty as Sally couldn't be expected to understand how dangerous she was and Lemuel would have to give up this whole affair. Beautiful black women were a curse; Peter had learned that from Lucy, his dead wife. Long before they married, while she was still nursing him back to life after the whipping that finally "broke" him, Lucy had explained that women on the farm had learned how to handle Master Van Roop, the overseer who had preceded Tucker.

"The onliest way," she'd said, "is t' let him take you the first time. If'n y'ain't too good lookin,' he'll just move on t' the next 'un. I's lucky he ain't took me but once."

Yes, pretty black women were dangerous, just like perfectly trained and beautiful black children. They would always be the most desirable to whites. They would always wind up breaking a black man's heart. Peter decided to bide his time until the spring planting began. Then, he'd have another serious conversation with Lemuel.

But winter seemed to hold the land in its solid, icy grip forever. Even the April rains were often mixed with snow. Then May remained colder than normal, and the ground would not yield to the plow until early June. Because planting had started so late, everyone was forced to work longer days to catch what was sure to be a shorter growing season. Daybreak found the slaves already in the fields, and the horn didn't blow again until after nightfall. The weary men and women barely had time get back to their cabins, eat and fall into their beds before they were being summoned again for the next day's work.

Peter's responsibilities as Tucker's unofficial assistant kept him even busier than the others. If the overseer was supervising the wheat fields, Peter was expected to make sure that corn or rye was being planted in the adjacent fields. Lemuel was somehow always either two fields over or assigned to some other detail for most of the planting time. Even when Peter made sure to specifically pick Lemuel to work with him, there was never a moment when was he was close enough to speak to him without being overheard by the others.

Summer finally took hold in July and the days blazed hot as harvest time began. Sally was, by now, beginning her sixth month. She made a visit to Mary and Zack's cabin one sultry afternoon when she knew Tucker would be in one of the fields farthest from the quarters. Zack's health had begun to fail during the winter and he spent most of his days in the cabin. Mary now watched all of the children, which allowed her to take care of Zack as well.

As soon as Sally appeared in the open doorway, a child toddled over to her, both arms raised. Sally picked Tom up and kissed him; she hugged her boy close, nuzzling both cheeks before setting him back down. Zack lay on a pallet near the fireplace. Even with the day's thick heat in the room, embers smoldered, sending up tiny licks of flame. Zack's emaciated body no longer generated enough heat and he needed a fire, even on the hottest of days. Sally came and sat beside him, little Tom still clinging to her skirt. She took up one of Zack's large, bony hands and laid it against her cheek. Zack regarded her quietly, his rheumy eyes kind, but curious.

"Who you?"

"Sally."

"Yer the gal what got Lemuel all upset an what."

"I ain't mean t'upset him. We just loves each other is all. Just like you an Mary."

Just then, Mary entered, surrounded by a mob of children; three of Sally's were among them. They were easy to pick out; Sarah, Zack and Simon were all a medium brown, with curly black hair. Even with their lighter skin, they all looked exactly like Sally, smooth-faced with wide-open brown eyes. The children stared at the stranger with the belly. None of Sally's other children recognized her, only Tom.

"All a you git on back outside now. "Cain't be disturbin' Uncle Zack. I be out directly."

Sarah tugged politely on Mary's skirt. "Aint Mary, who that?" She pointed to Sally, all the while hiding her face in the skirt's folds.

"Just never you mind." Mary leaned down close and whispered something in the child's ear. "Go on with the others now."

The little girl peeped out, smiled at Sally and then immediately helped usher the other children back outside.

"What'cha tell her?" Sally's arm instinctively circled Tom's little shoulders.

"Told her you her ma'am. So's she know she had a mama what couldn't keep her. Each a yer chil'ren gone know who they ma'am is. Even if'n they cain't never see her."

"Where Mary at?" Sally asked about her eldest. "How come she ain't with the others?"

"Given her a little job minding the hen house. She out there now collecting eggs."

Satisfied about the state of her children, Sally turned to the business at hand. "This one," she placed her free hand on her belly, "ain't Masta Tucker baby. It belong t' Lemuel."

Zack struggled to sit up, his face working. "Gal!" his shout came out as a croak, "What'cha done? You just killed that boy!"

Mary covered her mouth with both hands. Her eyes swam. "Oh, please Jesus! Say you ain't done it! How you git a baby by Lemuel? When you had the time? An how you know that baby in there ain't Masta Tucker own?"

Sally caught Mary's hands, pulled them against her own breast and held them fast. Not until that moment had she realized the full weight of what she'd done. It was just that she'd wanted a child with the man she loved! Was that so very wrong?

Mary pulled first one hand free, then the other. She wiped her eyes and reached for Tom. The little boy, sensing the fear in the room, had started to cry. She took the child on her lap.

"What'cha done, y' done. Ain't no use asking why or how. Just gotta figger out what t' do now. Masta Tucker cain't never see this chile if'n it come out black." Mary immediately got to her feet. "Go on back home now," she said at last, "I think I know what t' do."

She ushered Sally outside. Then she called the children to come get cleaned up.

CHAPTER 9

*O*n an unusually warm day early in October, Sally went into labor. It actually began just before sunrise, but she said nothing to Tucker. Instead, she got up as usual, made his coffee and began breakfast. Tucker rose shortly after her, drank the coffee and then ate a piece of cornbread before leaving the cabin. As soon as he was out of sight, Sally took the shortcut to the cabins. By the time she reached Mary and Zack's, the pains were very close together.

Mary had gotten up early as well. She spent the nights holding Zack in her arms, keeping him warm. They both knew their final separation was near and he seemed to appreciate the closeness of her body even more than her warmth. She'd come outside to relieve herself and was washing up when she saw the ungainly figure stumbling toward her.

"Sally!" Mary cried out, then whispered, "What'cha doing here?"

"It's time," Sally gasped. Her legs gave way and she fell.

Mary hurried to help her to her feet. For a moment, the older woman wondered why Sally had risked walking all the way to the cabins in her condition. Then she remembered.

"Gotta git'cha back 'fore Masta Tucker find out yer gone!"

They walked back to Tucker's cabin, Mary supporting Sally's every step. By now the pains were almost continuous and it was all Sally could do to keep from having the baby on the road. As soon as she got inside, she squatted and strained hard, just once. Mary got down too, very stiffly since her knees no longer tolerated such a position and was able to catch the infant just before it hit the floor. She turned the baby over and made the announcement.

"It's a girl!"

Sally had crawled to the bed and pulled herself up.

She gasped, "She black?"

"She black, alright." Mary answered, quickly washing the infant in a basin of water that Sally had left on the table. She wrapped her just as quickly and was about to hurry out of the door.

"Wait! Lemme see her!" Sally cried out, sitting upright reaching out for her child.

"You ain't gone have no time with this 'un. Name her quick! I gotta go!"

Mary brought the bundle over to the bed and lifted a corner of the cloth. A tiny head emerged, covered with tight black curls. The little black face was completely scrunched up.

"She name Polly, after my mama." Sally gently touched the bundle. "I'm a come 'round t' nurse her soon as I can."

Mary hurried out of the cabin. She ran with the infant all the way back to her own, where Zack was propped up on his pallet. He watched her enter, yellowed eyes too large for his nearly skeletal face.

"That Sally baby?" he whispered hoarsely. "What is it? It Lemuel own?"

"She a girl. An yeah, she Lemuel baby, alright."

The most important thing now was what to tell Tucker. Mary spoke quickly as she prepared a bed for the infant in a wooden crate.

"Got t' git back! Zack, can you watch her fer just a bit whilst I'm gone?"

"Go on, darlin'. Just slide her over by me. We be fine."

Mary placed the crate next to Zack's pallet. Then she hurried out of the cabin and ran up the road that led to Tucker's cabin. She quickly peeked inside, satisfying herself that Sally was still in bed and had, in fact, fallen asleep. Then, almost without pausing for breath, she hurried toward the nearest fields. Here workers were taking in a harvest of wheat. Men and women wielding scythes cut down the golden stalks that were quickly caught and bundled by the children, some as young as eight or nine. Tucker wasn't in this field, so Mary passed through quickly, hoping no one would notice her presence and question her being away from her charges.

She found Tucker in the next field over, standing atop a low stone wall watching the workers harvesting rye. Mary slowed to a walk, her mind busily constructing the tale she would tell the overseer. He didn't see her immediately, so she had time to get close enough to speak without raising her voice.

"Masta Tucker, sir, I just come from Sally, sir," she began, then stopped.

"Yeah? What? She had that baby?"

Tucker's eyes lit up and he grinned. He jumped down and grabbed Mary by the hand, forgetting he'd made it a rule never to touch any of the workers in a familiar way. This was his own child! His first!

"What she had?" he shouted, actually laughing aloud.

"Masta Tucker, sir, I got bad news this time."

Mary's words, so softly spoken, stopped Tucker cold. He dropped her hand and just stood there, still smiling crookedly. But inside, his stomach suddenly constricted.

"Whatcha mean, bad news? Sally alright, ain't she?"

"Yessir. It-it the babe. It didn't live. Yer baby borned dead, Masta."

Tucker's right arm twitched slightly as if to rise up of its own accord and strike down the bearer of this evil news. Mary, fully aware of the danger, knew she had no recourse other than to take the blow, if it came. A silent moment passed, and then another. Tucker made no movement; even his expression remained frozen – his smile becoming ever more grotesque.

At last, Mary broke the silence. "Masta Tucker, sir, you wanna see Sally? She had a hard time with this 'un, sir."

Her voice seemed to rouse the overseer. Tucker muttered, "Yeah, yeah," pushed past her and started off in the direction of his cabin. He didn't even bother to shout his usual warning to the workers about what he would do if he found out they had slacked off in his absence. Inside him, a sense of bitterness was growing, spreading storm clouds of rage throughout his chest and belly. Why? Why couldn't this have happened to one of Sally's other babies? Why to *his*? What had he done wrong? What had she?

"Mary!" Tucker shouted suddenly, turning partly around to address the woman just behind him, "Sally come see you whilst she was carrying this 'un?"

"No sir, Masta. Last time she come was t' drop off that baby she had 'fore this 'un."

"She ain't show no sickness this time? 'Fore this 'un were borned?"

"It were the quickest delivery so far, Masta. Sally ain't had no trouble I could see."

"Thought you said she had a hard time."

Mary quickly caught herself. "After, Masta Tucker. The birthing were'nt the hard part. It were finding out 'bout the babe dying. That what upset her so."

Tucker had slowed his pace only slightly during this exchange. Now he turned back in the direction of his cabin and lengthened his stride considerably. Mary couldn't keep up. He reached the open doorway well ahead of her.

Sally was in his bed, apparently asleep. Tucker stepped inside and approached the bed as quietly as he could. Even so, she stirred and suddenly opened her eyes; they were filled with fear.

"Masta Tucker, I'm sorry," her voice quavered, rose and then broke. "I know'd you was counting on this 'un. I done everything just like all the other times."

Tucker, seeing her tears, knew he should try to offer her some comfort. But instead he blurted out, "Goddammit, Sally! You done had five live chil'ren fer the master a this place! I go an buy you, spend five year's worth a wages on you, an you cain't even give me m' own chile!"

He turned on his heel and nearly collided with Mary, who'd finally reached the cabin door.

"Woman!" he bellowed, "Git the hell outta my way!" He stormed past her out the door and headed back toward the fields.

"He ain't hurt 'cha none, did he?" Mary whispered as she tip-toed to Sally's bedside, as though Tucker were still somewhere nearby.

"No," Sally sounded almost gleeful, "He might just beat me later on, just t' remind me who I belong to. "Don't care if'n he do! I done what I set out t' do. He cain't change that!"

Mary couldn't share Sally's sense of triumph. "That babe y' just had, she ain't gone be safe if'n y' tries t' be her Ma. An Lemuel cain't claim her neither. All y' done was t' spite Masta Tucker. That's all y' done, chile."

"That ain't why I done it. Was t' give me an Lemuel somebody belongs t' us. I know I cain't have Polly, Lemuel neither. But she here! An she ourn. I done gave up all m' other chil'ren. Just gone have t' give this 'un up sooner, is all."

The speech seemed to take the last of Sally's strength. She'd been sitting up, arms wrapped almost protectively around herself. Suddenly, she lay back and closed her eyes. Mary watched Sally drift off to sleep. She pulled the thin blanket up beneath the young woman's chin, gently smoothed the worn fabric and then tiptoed out of the cabin, quietly closing the door behind her.

CHAPTER 10

*P*olly was a good baby who almost never made much noise. Even her hungry cries were soft, like the mewling of a newborn kitten. Nonetheless, Sally seemed to know exactly when her daughter absolutely had to be fed. No sooner would the soft whimpers begin, when Sally would appear at Mary and Zack's shack. Even in the middle of the night, Sally came to nurse Polly, quietly slipping in and going to the wooden cradle that Mary kept right by the door. Sometimes, because she rarely slept much anyway, Mary would hear the cradle creak faintly as Sally lifted Polly and settled with her on the dirt floor. Mary would neither speak nor otherwise indicate that she was awake. All too soon these visits would have to end, but for now, she wanted Sally to have as much precious time alone with her daughter as possible.

In those first few weeks after giving birth, Sally would disguise herself in order to slip into and out of the slave quarters unnoticed. She did so by wearing some of Tucker's old clothes. He'd kept several shirts and pairs of trousers from his youth that no longer fit him and, because the fabric was still good, it made sense to expect Sally to let out the seams and remake the garments for him. So she wore one of his too-small shirts and a pair of the trousers as her disguise. With her thick wooly hair covered by one of Tucker's wide brimmed straw hats and in her bare feet, she could pass for a teenage boy sent from the fields on an errand.

Nevertheless, the whispering began almost immediately, even though Mary did her best to keep the details about the overseer's last child vague. All she would say to anyone who asked was, "It were borned dead. Buried it myself."

Starved for a story, folk quickly began to embellish the bare bones of Mary's tale. Someone started a rumor that the child had been born deformed and that Tucker had ordered it killed.

"Naw!" A worker in the fields whispered, "What I heard, this 'un were borned too black! Favor'd the ma! That why he had it killed!"

Of course, the various rumors soon reached Peter. He instinctively knew not to believe most of them, except the one about the baby's color. If this child were Lemuel's, of course it would have been black. And Peter didn't think for one minute that Mary would have let it die. No! Peter was almost certain that the child was alive and that Tucker didn't know it. Lemuel was now in real danger, Peter realized. The young man simply had to give up the whole affair with Sally and Peter would see to it. He had only to get proof that Sally's baby still lived.

Peter resumed his late night walks through the slave quarters, being careful always to keep to the shadows. He knew that several women had recently given birth, so he passed by their shanties over the first few nights and peeped into their windows. Everyone's shutters were still open during this unusually warm spell and he was able to count the mothers and babies; one had given birth to twins. However, he found no extra infants with any of those families, so Sally's babe wasn't with them. Next he went by Mary and Zack's cabin. All of Sally's children lived there, but Peter had no real idea of how many there were. And, in spite of the glow from their fireplace, Peter couldn't see into the room well enough to tell if an infant was there.

On the fifth night, as Peter hid behind a corner of the single men's shack, he espied a figure lurking near the door. A moment later, Lemuel slipped out and the two disappeared into the gloom of the forest behind the shack. Peter waited for nearly two hours, until he saw Lemuel reappear and quietly reenter the shanty. A moment later, the figure stepped into clear moonlight–barefoot, clad in a rough shirt and trousers, and wearing a straw hat. Peter wasn't fooled by the disguise. He hadn't seen the girl since she was taken by Tucker six years ago. But it was Sally; he was sure of it.

"Missy!" Peter moved out of the shadows and called to her. "You need t' stop right where yer at."

Sally froze. She had no idea who this man was, but she knew she'd been caught in the worst possible way. The man had clearly seen through her attempted cover.

"Missy, I just need t' talk t' you. I ain't gone hurt you – nor any a' yorn."

"Wh-who're you?"

"Name's Peter, Missy. Don't know yer name, but I knows who y' are. You Masta Tucker woman, ain't cha."

"Sally. My name's Sally. An yeah, Masta Tucker taken me fer his own." Sally squared her shoulders and raised her chin, almost defiantly. "I ain't picked him. It weren't no choice a mine!"

Peter snorted, "Gal! where you git off talking 'bout 'picking'? Purty black woman like yerself don't git t' pick if'n the ovaseer decide t' take you!"

At his words, Sally seemed to sink into herself, weighted down by their stark reality. After a long silent moment, she spoke without raising her head.

"What cha want, Mista Peter, sir?"

"Want cha t' let that boy Lemuel go. He cain't have you an' you cain't have him. All you's doin' is gittin' yerselfs in more trouble. How long you think Masta Tucker gone stay blind t' what's going on? If'n I could find out, don't cha think he gone find out one day too? An when he do, he gone whip the hide off'a the both a you."

Peter paused, giving Sally time to digest what he'd just said. Then he continued, "Course there's also that babe y' just birthed, the one everybody think be dead. It ain't dead is it? How come y' hidin' it from Masta Tucker? Cause it black? That it?"

Sally nearly fainted. Her knees buckled and she swayed momentarily. Peter caught her with a steadying hand, and then held her fast, his fingers vice-like around her wrist.

"You let the boy go an I ain't never gone say nothin' more 'bout cha babe. Y' got it hid good enough. An Masta Tucker he don't know one lil' nigger babe from another 'un. It'll be safe."

So, it had come at last – the moment Sally had been dreading ever since the first day on this farm. She'd always known that somehow Lemuel would finally be taken from her. Nonetheless, she wasn't prepared for Peter's words. They pierced her literally taking away her ability to breathe. Living every day with Master Tucker, having him take her night after night and no Lemuel to go to for real love, was simply not possible.

But then she thought of Polly who had to be protected. Sally had no other choice. For a full beat, she strained to find breath enough to say what she needed.

"Mista Peter," she finally whispered fighting back tears, " I'ma do like you say, sir. If'n you swear true you ain't gone say nothin' 'bout no babe t' Masta Tucker, I swear true I ain't never gone see Lemuel no more."

Peter had been watching Sally's face closely as she spoke, looking for signs of deception. After all, beautiful women were natural deceivers; they couldn't help themselves. They were always being pursued by men, black and white alike. Lucy used to say that these women *had* to lie, either to the black men they loved or to the white men who wanted them. But at this moment, Sally's anguish seemed real enough. And so Peter released her wrist and took a step back.

"I gotcha word then?" he muttered.

Sally nodded, no longer able to speak. Abruptly, she whirled and ran off. The woods' darkness swallowed her retreat.

CHAPTER 11

For the next few weeks, Lemuel waited each night for Sally. Lying on the floor in his thin blanket amidst the other men, he strained to hear her low whistle. As the weeks became a month, and then another, he first became worried, and then frantic. Finally he decided to speak his fears to Mary. He was sure that Sally was still visiting her and Zack's cabin to nurse Polly. Perhaps he could even catch her there, if he waited until after nightfall.

Mary and Zack's cabin bustled with the activity of children. During the workday, from just before dawn until sundown, fifty black youngsters, all less than seven years old, crowded into the single room. Those who couldn't get inside, spilled out onto the dust-covered area in front of the cabin. The grounds around all the workers' shacks had been trodden bare of grass by the comings and goings of so many weary feet. Dust hung perpetually in the air, and all the children ended their days covered in a fine film of it. Mary would not let any of the children go home dirty; she filled her washtub and bathed them before settling them down to wait for their parents.

Lemuel arrived in the midst of Mary's bath-time ministrations. Zack, being awake less and less these days, was already asleep on their pallet beside the fireplace. Mercifully, the sickness that was slowly consuming his body seemed to be causing him very little pain. Usually, when Lemuel came for his evening meal, he avoided even looking at the cradle that held his daughter. But this time, as soon as he'd stepped through the door, he headed directly to it. For the very first time, he lifted the infant tentatively and held her with one hand under her head and the other under her behind, his arms held out at stiff angles like a bird's wings. Mary looked up from drying off a naked, wriggling child, pulled a rough woolen shirt over his head, and sent him to lie down with the others. Then she approached Lemuel.

"Here, lemme show you how t' hold her. You got t' be natural with chil'ren. Just hold her close t' you. Like that."

Mary rearranged Lemuel's arms so that the baby's head lay in the crook of his bent elbow, her body supported by both his arms. He gazed down at his child, trying to see Sally in the small, scrunched-up face.

"Sally say she told you 'bout how this be my chile." Lemuel spoke hesitantly. He'd said nothing about the baby's birth to her until this moment.

"Oh yeah. She say it yorn." Mary fixed Lemuel with a momentarily hard glare. "But I knowed it weren't yer fault. Sally—well…." Mary let her voice trail off. After all, what was the use of blaming either of them.

Lemuel stood silently holding the baby for several minutes. Just as Mary was about to return to her charges, he spoke up again without looking in her direction.

"Miz Mary, has you seen Sally? Is she alright?"

"Why, yea. She come just this evening t'nurse Polly. What, you ain't seen her?"

"No ma'am. Ain't seen her fer the longest." Lemuel stared at the ground as he spoke, ashamed to meet Mary's eyes.

"Well, Son, Sally know what she can do and what she cain't. If'n she ain't able t' see you, y' just got t' bide by that." Mary gave Lemuel a stern look as she took Polly out of his arms and laid the infant in her cradle. She started to say something more, then thought better of it. After a moment she spoke again.

"Go on over t' the fire an git 'cher supper. The pot's still hot."

Lemuel knew Mary would give him no more information. In fact, he now feared that she'd never mention Sally again, nor allow him to speak about her either.

CHAPTER 12

S ometimes, Peter still had bad dreams. Before Lucy had finally gotten pregnant again, he had nightmares about the terrible day when they lost their three children. Young as he was, little Paul had tried to be brave, telling Peter, "I'm a take care a' Peggy an Jenny, Pa." But the two little girls had cried so hard, clinging to their mother's skirt, as Peter, on his knees in the dirt had pleaded with Master Tucker to send him off–do anything but separate his children from their mother.

Of course, there was nothing else that could be done. Tucker had at least made sure the wagon carrying the children was out of sight before taking his whip to Peter; after all, such bitter complaints from a slave couldn't go unpunished. However, sending off those children seemed to have hurt the overseer almost as much as it had Peter. But, there was no way he could've have said so. It would have meant siding with a slave over the master. What Tucker had done, instead, was to favor Peter by making him his right hand man and giving him control over the other workers.

For his part, Peter had cared nothing for the favor. In fact, he hated Tucker with a white-hot intensity that could have gotten him into danger. But he'd masked his feelings expertly from everyone except Lucy.

After the children were gone, Lucy would always remind Peter that there had to be the hope of a reunion in the next world, if not in this one. Out of love, he would never dispute her, although he himself held no such belief. All his faith lay solely in Lucy. She was the single reason he was still alive. When dreams of that awful day would awaken him in tears, his only comfort was in her arms.

Lucy would continually warn Peter that no hatred could truly remain secret. "Husband," she would say, "You got t' let it go. We in this life t' suffer sometimes. An us black folk always got t' take our losses. But there's a brighter day on the other side. You just got t' keep yer heart pure from sin. Hatin' Masta Tucker, that just sinful! Even if'n don't nobody else know, God know! Jesus know! Please, Peter, please let it go!"

At first, Lucy's last pregnancy had eased their grief. But then, she began to have dizzy spells when she was working in the fields. When Peter found her unconscious in one of the corn fields and carried her to Tucker, the overseer had allowed her to remain in her cabin until the baby was born.

Mary had assisted with the birth and she'd also witnessed Lucy's last breaths. To Mary, it was as though the mother had passed her own life into her infant daughter. Lucy closed her eyes and was, quite simply, no more. When Mary came outside carrying the baby, Peter realized immediately that something had gone terribly wrong. He charged into the cabin, snatched up his wife and tried to wake her. His howls brought Zack and most of the other workers, all of whom tried to get him to release his powerful grip on Lucy. But Peter simply wouldn't let her go; in fact, he threatened to kill anyone who tried to take her away from him.

Zack hadn't yet had his crippling injury and was much taller and stronger than anyone else on the farm. He simply took hold of Peter from behind and with one arm around Peter's neck, applied just enough pressure to make him pass out. Zack then carried Peter out of the cabin, so that Mary and several other women could go inside to wash, dress and wrap Lucy's body in an improvised shroud made of the blanket that had covered her.

Zack had had to restrain Peter throughout the night's burial. The desperate man's screams were so loud that Tucker had heard them in his cabin and had come to investigate. The overseer kept his distance however, watching the burial proceedings from a field adjacent to the slaves' graveyard.

For more than a few years afterward, Peter could not wake up each morning without wishing that death had come for him during the night. Only a promise made to Lucy at the start of that last pregnancy had kept him from taking his own life.

"I'm older 'n you." she'd said. "If'n I was t' go first. You got t' promise t' take care a our babe."

Peter had simply hugged her tightly, telling her, "Don't talk such awfulness. You gone bury me."

Lucy would not be put off. She'd insisted on hearing him say it. And so he finally had. That promised was all that had kept him tethered to this world and their last child.

However, for months after Lucy's death, Peter couldn't even bear to look at the baby, much less name her. He'd let Mary take her, since Mary had given birth during that year and still had her milk. Nonetheless, his vow had haunted him without relief.

Finally, one night about a year later, he'd forced himself to walk down the row of shacks to Mary and Zack's. Without entering, he'd called softly to Mary.

"Sorry t' come by so late, but I'm a take m' daughter home now. I done left her on you too long already."

Mary had come to the door wearing only her shift. Rubbing her eyes, she'd peered out into the darkness trying to make out who had come by at such an hour. Everyone inside was sleeping soundly; the horn would be sounding before daybreak, and each hour spent in rest was precious.

"That you, Peter?" she'd whispered, "How come you ain't git by earlier? Yer babe 'sleep now."

"Sorry," Peter muttered, "You right, I shoulda come by 'fore now. But I got t' take her now I'm here."

Mary had disappeared into the gloom and reappeared holding the baby, draped over one shoulder, still quite asleep. Wordlessly, she'd transferred the child to Peter. The little girl had immediately wrapped both arms around her father's neck and pulled her little legs up against his chest. He'd felt the sweet weight of her body, rested his cheek against her soft wooly hair. And in that moment, he knew her name had to be Lucy.

Peter found himself reliving these painful memories for several days after his encounter with Sally. He told himself that he'd done the right thing, the best thing for all concerned. Lemuel would get over Sally once he was married to Lucy. After all, Lucy had been able to heal her father's heart—something Peter would never have believed possible. The girl had her mother's tender spirit; Lemuel could not help but learn to love her. All that remained was convincing Lemuel to accept reality. Sally could not belong to him and they could no longer have their nighttime trysts.

And Sally, well, she would just have to make the best of her lot, knowing her child was safe. Peter was, after all, a man of his word. He would make certain that no one could ever raise any questions about Sally's *black baby*.

CHAPTER 13

*O*ne month went by, then another. The work was now in full swing in preparation for the winter harvest. Men and women spent all the daylight hours cutting rye, wheat and corn.

Lemuel worked almost mechanically. He took no breaks, often forgetting even to stop for water. When the horn finally blew sometime after sunset, he'd shoulder his scythe and follow the others out of whichever field they'd been working. Instead of heading over to Mary and Zack's for his supper, he'd go straight to the men's shack, throw himself down on his blanket and let sleep either find or elude him. Something awful must have happened to Sally for her to cut him off like this and there was no way for him to find out what that could be. Whenever he could spot Master Tucker, Lemuel would try to get close enough to the overseer to watch him. Had the man found out about Polly? Was that why Sally could not get out any more? Tucker did seem a bit meaner than usual, but the gossip among the workers was that the overseer was just mad about the death of his last child.

"Word is the ovaseer taken his own coin t' buy the wench what live with him. So's them chil'ren what she have now belongs t' him. Bet he takin' the loss a this 'un pretty hard!"

None of the gossipers showed much pity for the overseer's plight. There was general chuckling – all quite surreptitious, of course, as the speakers shared their reliably-gotten tale. In fact, it was Peter who had started the story, making sure the baby's death was its prominent feature. Everyone believed if Peter said something about Master Tucker, it was gospel truth.

Lemuel alone knew the story wasn't true, at least the part about the death. Even so, it took him the full two months to realize Peter was spreading a lie that protected Polly, which meant that Peter had to know about Sally.

This realization hit Lemuel late one night as he lay awake amidst the other snoring men. He struggled with the thoughts now sweeping in on him. How long had Peter known that he and Sally were meeting? Had he, Peter, actually spied on them as they made love? And, worst of all, why hadn't Peter told Master Tucker, since the overseer clearly trusted him so much?

By the time the horn blew, Lemuel had everything figured out. He now understood that Peter intended to use Polly's safety to force him to marry Lucy. And Peter must have gotten to Sally as well; of course she would stop seeing Lemuel to protect their daughter. Lemuel had never before experienced the rage that suddenly consumed him – a sickening, helpless rage.

Even when Sally was taken that first day, as upset and angry as he was, his feelings were tempered by resignation. It was no one's fault except the overseer's, and everybody knew there was nothing a black man could do about that. But this was altogether a different matter! Peter had done this – had used a secret between lovers that had nothing to do with anyone else to get what he wanted!

Lemuel wondered, as he rose, folded his blanket and joined the other workers outside, how soon Peter would approach him again with his offer. He wasn't sure he would be able to refrain from knocking the man down as soon as he saw him.

"Devil done woke you up this morning? You means t' scare the chile?" The man who spoke was standing beside Lemuel drinking from a dipper of water.

A fair skinned girl with curly black hair was circulating among the assembled workers, offering each a morning drink. Now she stood squarely in front of Lemuel. She'd offered the dipper to him first, but had backed away when she saw his scowl.

Lemuel caught himself. He had to control his feelings, now more than ever. He quickly forced a smile. "Sorry 'bout the bad face. Thank "ee chile. Ain't mean t' scare you."

He took the dipper from his neighbor, dipped out some water, drank and handed it back to the girl. Something about her look made him pause.

"What 'cha name chile?" Lemuel asked.

"Mary." She smiled as she said it, a dimple appearing under her left eye.

Lemuel's heart skipped. This had to be one of Sally's children. She so resembled her mother. Although he'd been taking meals at Mary and Zack's for over five years, he'd never let himself notice any of Sally's children, even though he knew they were there. Now, suddenly, he wished he could stand still and gaze at this child all day. He could feel the heat of his rage cooling under her steady gaze.

"You got 'cha a nice name, Mary," Lemuel's smile was genuine now. "Hope I see you tomorrow."

"You will. This my new job now." Mary said proudly, sticking out her small chest.

That day passed without Lemuel setting eyes on Peter. This gave him more time to calm down and think. As he cut and bundled wheat, his mind and heart flew to Sally. No longer could he afford to ache for even the briefest meeting with her now he ached for what she had to be suffering in his absence. She'd told him, all too often, how the only way she could stomach Master Tucker was in knowing that sometimes, she could be with the one she truly loved.

How could he, Lemuel, even consider belonging to someone else while Sally had to live out her life in misery? The day ended with him well past exhaustion and no closer to a solution.

CHAPTER 14

*T*hat night, long after the children had been fed, bathed and returned to their parents, and after her own and Sally's children were all in bed, Mary finally lay her weary body down next to Zack. He stirred as she pulled him close. His body was cool against her warmth.

"Darlin'," his cracked voice whispered, "wish't you didn't have t' work so hard. Know you tired."

"Well, the bed feel real good now I'm here. Go on t' sleep, Zack."

Just before first light, Mary awakened to a distinct chill all around her body. Pulling back the blankets with her free hand, she discovered the source. Some time after they'd spoken, Zack had slipped from sleep into death, his arms still wrapped tightly around her, just like every other night of their life together.

His body was now cold and in full rigor. Mary fought the impulse to cry out in panic. Luke, their eldest, would be coming by soon to check on his parents before heading out to the fields. He would be able to pry his father's arms apart enough to release her. In the intervening half-light, Mary gazed down at Zack's face. He looked peaceful – no, more than peaceful – beatific, almost joyful.

Thank you, sweet Jesus. You took him easy, she thought, tears gathering and spilling down her cheeks.

Because it was Zack, and Mary was so important to the workers with children, Tucker allowed an hour off during that morning for Zack's burial. Mary, herself bathed and shrouded Zack's
body; she would let no one else help her but Luke. He straightened his father's rail-thin limbs and crossed the large bony hands
over the sunken chest. Together, they wrapped Zack's body in one
of his blankets. Only when his face was covered did Mary allow
the rest of her children to come to the bedside and bid their father
farewell.

The workers all assembled outside the cabin as Zack's sons carried his body out, followed by Mary, their daughters and all her
small charges, each one wearing a somber expression. Without
fully understanding what was going on, the children all took their
cues from Mary. Her tearstained face was at the same time both
sad and triumphant.

At the graveside, Lemuel found himself standing one worker
away from Peter. Just as he was adjusting to this fact, Lemuel
caught sight of Sally. Tucker had come to watch the burial and,
amazingly, had allowed her to attend as well. Of course, she stood
well away from the other workers. Lemuel forced himself to keep
his eyes fixed on Mary. He was keenly aware that Peter was watching him and Sally alert to any hint that they were in contact with
one another.

There was no one on the farm, other than Zack who knew
any of the Dutch Reform prayers. In fact, burials were the only
opportunities for any semblance of worship, since Tucker had
neither knowledge of nor inclination toward providing any reli-
gious services for the workers. Once Zack became ill, Mary did
her best, adapting some of the prayers she'd heard Zack recite and
creating her own. Still, that seemed too much to ask of her this
morning, so one of the older men named Quash stepped forward
and improvised a prayer, drawing freely upon snatches of phrases

he'd heard from Zack and Mary. Dutch had been Quash's first language; he'd never really mastered English.

"Dear Lord, 'ere lie Yer good an faithful servant, Zack, what have serv-ed Yer Holy Name all 'is life. Now 'ee dead an needin' Yer mercy, Lord. Take 'im up unto Yer bosom an fit 'im wit the wings like one 'a Yer angels. Amen."

The service completed, the workers gathered into two work gangs, leaving three men to dig Zack's grave. Lemuel stepped forward as one of the three, grabbing a shovel and leaning into the task. Tucker took charge of the largest gang and led them off. Peter glanced at Lemuel briefly, then went to the head of the second gang and marched them off in the opposite direction. When Lemuel finally looked up from the open grave, Sally was nowhere in sight.

CHAPTER 15

*W*atching Zack's burial, even from a distance proved to be almost more than Sally could bear. As soon as Lemuel stepped out from the crowd and began to dig, she whirled and ran back to the cabin. Once inside, she collapsed on the floor in tears. She was still crying hard when Tucker came in for his morning meal.

"Sally, gal," he moaned, "You got t' git over this! I knowed I was wrong fer blamin' you 'bout the babe. Jest made you more upset, what I done, an I'm sorry fer that. But, listen. The next 'un, it'll be fine. You'll see."

He pulled her roughly into his arms. Giving comfort did feel so terribly awkward to him, but she'd been crying almost continually for weeks. Sally allowed the embrace but didn't return it. When, after a moment, she pulled away, Tucker completely lost his patience.

"Dammit, Sally! He shouted. "I said I was sorry! What more d' you want outta me? T' were my loss too!"

When, instead of answering, she simply stared at him with tear-filled eyes, he slammed out of the cabin, leaving the food on the table untouched.

Sally rushed out after him. "Masta! Wait!" she cried, running hard now to catch up.

Tucker heard her. He stopped but didn't turn around. Sally faced him with hands clasped as though in prayer.

"Masta, it's more'n just losin' my babe. I still got milk. I need t' give it t' some other woman's babe, else I'm a git sick!"

"Well, why ain't cha say so 'fore now?" Tucker breathed in relief. "I'm 'a git Mary up here right away! She can bring you a babe t' nurse. There's got t' be a new one in that passel a' lil' niggers she keep." Tucker took Sally's arm and walked her back to the cabin. "You jest wait here."

Sally scraped the cornmeal mush back into the pot to keep warm on the grate. She prayed that Mary would recognize this opportunity and bring Polly to Sally to nurse. In this way, she would no longer have to sneak around, risking an encounter with either Peter – or Lemuel. And, as Peter had noted, Tucker, doubtless, couldn't tell one black baby from another. He shouldn't connect Polly to Sally, as long as Peter kept his word.

About an hour later, a knock came on the open door frame; it was Mary carrying a bundle. Sally gestured for her to come inside. Reaching for the swaddled infant, Sally carefully removed the blanket. Polly immediately began searching for milk, turning her head against Sally's breast and opening her tiny mouth,

"You's one smart gal, I give you that!" Mary exclaimed, sitting wearily on the bench beside Tucker's wooden table. Only her reddened eyes revealed the depths of her recent ordeal. "How you got Masta Tucker t' come an order me t' bring you the 'newest-borned' babe I got, well…"

Sally gazed down on her daughter, now nursing lustily. "Jest told him I had t' git rid a my milk. You the smart one. T' were your story kept Polly safe." Sally looked up, tears filled her eyes. "I'm so sorry 'bout Zack. He were such a good man. I'm a miss him."

"He better off where he at now," Mary sighed, "'Where the evil cease from troublin' an the weary be at rest.'"

After a moment, Sally spoke again, this time very tentatively. "Mary, I had t' break off seein' Lemuel. It 'bout t' kill me, but it the onliest way t' keep Masta Tucker from findin' out 'bout Polly."

Mary absently rubbed the table top, her right hand following the grain of the wood. Her words, when they finally came, were reluctant as well.

"Somebody found out? Who?"

"Mista Peter. He spied on me an Lemuel fer long enough t' find out 'bout Polly. Then, he made me promise not t' ever see Lemuel no more, else he tell Masta Tucker the whole tale."

Another long silence followed. Neither the still very-young mother nor the much older widow could meet the other's eyes. At last, Mary spoke.

"Peter ain't a bad man. It wrong what he doin' t' you an Lemuel – wrong an hurtful. But, you can be sure he think he got a good reason fer doin' it. Did he tell you why?"

"Say Masta Tucker were bound t' find out one day an whip the both a us."

"He probably right 'bout that."

Suddenly Sally said, "Mista Peter don't know me. He think he do, but he don't. I given him my word on Lemuel an I means t' keep it. But that don't mean I'm a live out my days as Masta Tucker slave just t' give him one babe after another un!"

Something in Sally's flat, hardened voice put Mary on alert. The girl was nothing, if not determined. Was it possible that she was trying to figure out how to stop having any more children for Master Tucker?

"Sally, listen." Mary cautioned, "Some things y' cain't change. You was borned pretty an Masta Tucker taken' you. That you cain't do nothin' 'bout. You gone git t' nurse Polly, at least fer a while. An you won't have t' give up no more a yer chil'ren. We don't git t' pick the lives we was borned t' live. We just got t' live 'um."

Polly had finished nursing and Sally had placed the baby against her shoulder, gently patting her back until Polly burped. Rising, she transferred her daughter to Mary's arms and smiled weakly.

"Mary, you the best friend I got. 'An I'm a study on what 'cha tellin' me. You ain't got t' worry no more 'bout me. I done what was needed. Now I'm a try an make the best a things."

She watched Mary carry her daughter down the road toward the shanties. Truly, she wanted to avoid lying to Mary, but, she wasn't sure that she actually could go on without Lemuel. And she feared that he couldn't be without her either.

That night, for the first time, Sally was unable to muster even a pretense of ardor. Tucker worked feverishly for over an hour, trying to wring some pleasure out of the act of lovemaking. When, finally frustrated, he shouted an obscenity at her she burst into tears and refused to be comforted. After another hour of trying to sooth her, Tucker gave up, turned his back on her and went to sleep.

CHAPTER 16

*O*ver the next few days, Tucker discovered he was more upset by Sally's changed behavior than he cared to admit, even to himself. What could possibly be wrong with the girl that she was giving him so much grief? He realized, now, that he'd allowed his temper to get the better of him on more than one occasion, but Sally had never seemed to hold it against him before. Besides, she was *his servant* now, not just the woman selected to share his bed. Didn't she understand what that meant? He could, after all, punish her in any way he wished.

But, of course, he knew that wasn't going to be possible. Sally had such a hold on him that all he could think of was getting her to act like his lover again. It became a constant undercurrent, even as he tended to the details of preparing for the coming winter. Carrying around such unfamiliar emotions made him even angrier than usual and, not surprisingly, he turned the full weight of that anger on the slaves.

Two men, laboring amidst the bundles of wheat, shortly after sunset, grumbled to each other under their breaths.

"Masta Tucker done got the devil in him fer sure. Look how he got us workin' an the sun done gone down. Body cain't hardly see t' tie up the sheaves. Think he still mad 'bout that babe?"

"Betcha he is! Folk's sayin' how that gal a his were a good breeder right up 'til she carryin' his own chile. They sayin' how it real queer she losin' this 'un. Somethin' musta happened t' her. She supposed t'be a real pretty gal. Mebbe one a the mens taken a likin' t' her an tried somethin'."

"Naw! Would'nt no nigger dare t' touch her!"

"One or 'nother young buck might try."

Neither worker noticed the overseer had stopped just behind the row of not-yet cut wheat where they were working. Tucker had been about to shout a directive when he'd heard the drift of their conversation. He remained silent, listening intently. This, he had never considered, that Sally could have been attacked by someone, someone who would actually rape a pregnant woman! But why wouldn't she have told him if this, in fact, had happened?

The gal 'd be too scared t' say nothin'. "Feared I'd blame her fer being so careless, he thought. No wonder she was behaving so strangely.

The idea of a rape, once planted, quickly took root in the overseer's mind. Tucker became convinced this was what had happened and he now thought of little else. Who would have dared such a thing? He would find the scurrilous black dog and whip him within an inch of his life!

But finding the culprit wasn't going to be easy. These niggers couldn't be trusted to tell him who the guilty man was. He'd have to go to Peter. Peter would know how to get the truth out of them.

The relationship between the two men had never been comfortable for Tucker. It wasn't that Peter ever behaved in even a subtly disrespectful manner. The man followed every order Tucker gave, even anticipated orders he'd yet to think of. It was something else, a nagging sense of unease bordering on shame that came over him whenever he had to spend more than a few minutes alone with Peter. This meant that, over the years, he and Peter had actually had fewer than half a dozen actual conversations.

Still the matter had to be dealt with, and promptly. By now, the perpetrator probably thought he'd gotten away with his crime! He was, no doubt, even bragging about it to the other workers. More important than the rape was the fact that this scoundrel had made a fool of the overseer – and was continuing to do so!

Once he'd made the decision, Tucker sent one of the workers to find Peter and deliver a message: Tucker wanted to see him as soon as that day's work was finished. The two men met by a gnarled ancient oak at the beginning of the road leading down to the workers' shacks.

"Somethin' you want me t' do, Masta?" Peter wiped dirt from his hands and face with his kerchief as he spoke.

Tucker took a breath before saying, "Got a problem I need fer you t' handle." He paused again before continuing, "One a the boys taken liberties wit' m' woman. Want cha t' find out who done it an let me know."

Peter raised his eyes to a point just below Tucker's shirt collar – the closest he could safely come to looking a white man in the face. He chose his words carefully.

"Masta Tucker, sir. I am surely sorry t' hear that. Most surely sorry. Did y' gal say that what happened t' her, sir?"

Tucker was momentarily flustered. Why was Peter asking him this particular question? Sudden anger spurred his heartbeat, spreading a deep flush across his face that was visible even in the moonlight. He almost spit out a retort, but bit it off at the last moment.

Instead, with great effort he composed himself before saying calmly, "I knows m' woman. That's what happened. What I need is fer you t' find the nigger an tell me who it is. Cain't let somethin' like that happen an don't nobody git punished fer it. You got cha a daughter; y' ought t' be able t' understand what I'm sayin'."

Peter dropped his eyes. "Yessir, Masta Tucker. I surely do understand. I'm a git right t' it. Anythin' else Masta Tucker, sir? "

"No. You can go."

Tucker watched the man head off toward the shacks. His heart was still pumping heavily. Sally. God! He did want her so badly! But, more importantly, for the first time, he desperately wanted her to actually want him! For he realized, now, that Sally had never really approached him with desire. Yes, she always did whatever he asked and submitted to all his sexual demands, but he now suspected that she didn't truly care for him the way he cared for her. That thought, coupled with the suspicion of rape only served to further fuel his anger. The fact was the overseer had no idea how to win Sally's love.

By the time he'd reached his cabin, Tucker was more worked up then ever. Frustration almost caused him to shout for her until he had a sudden realization. Instead of giving in to his rage, he called out gently, "Sally 'I'm home."

She had her back to the door, lifting the iron kettle out of the grate. Turning around, she quickly brought his tin plate and mug to the table.

"Yer supper's ready, Masta. I'll bring you water t' wash up wit."

Sally was about to rush past him to fetch the dipper. Tucker caught her arm. She flinched. He loosened his grip immediately.

"If'n you ain't ate 'chet," he said softly, "git 'cha a plate an join me."

"I ate a lil' bit. Ain't real hungry right now."

"Then, I ain't neither." Tucker continued, somewhat hesitantly, "Can I just be wit'cha fer a bit?"

Immediately, Sally took off her apron and began to untie her skirt. Tucker stopped her.

"Naw, gal, I ain't askin' t' go t' bed. I just wanna sit an hold you a lil' while."

He lifted her in his arms and carried her over to the only wooden armchair. Placing her on his lap, Tucker drew Sally close. She leaned against his chest somewhat stiffly, causing him to force down yet another surge of anger, this time coupled with the all-too familiar rush of desire.

He was in completely unfamiliar territory now. Unsure what to do next, he kissed her suddenly, something he had never done except in the heat of lovemaking. Sally's lips were among her best features. Tucker realized, with surprise, how sweetly satisfying just kissing them could be. He did it again. And yet again. Each time was lovelier than the last. Finally, he simply let his heart guide him. He could feel it skipping and thumping wildly against her body.

Amazingly, Sally's arms wound themselves around his neck; she was actually returning his kisses! He was about to let himself go, sweep her up and throw her onto his bed when a small voice in his head stopped him.

Take yer time. Don't rush like y' always do.

Tucker heeded this warning. Moving gently, he stood Sally on her feet and rose from his chair. For a full moment they faced each other. Sally's eyes were closed, her face a beautiful immobile mask. Suddenly, she literally threw herself against his chest. He caught her up and carried her over to the bed. Still moving as slowly as he could manage, he undressed her and then himself. He took his time be-ginning the lovemaking, even as his whole body was urging him to speed things along. And Sally responded. For the first time, Tucker could actually sense that she was there with him, moving with him.

"Oh, Sally," he moaned, completely overwhelmed, "Sally, gal, d' ya love me? Say ya love me like I love you! Oh, Gal! You the sweetest thing in this whole world!"

The morning light warmed her eyelids until they finally yielded and opened. For just a few moments, Sally let that warmth envelope her – arms, legs, the woolen coverlet, all wrapped around her body. Then it struck her like a thunderclap! Master Tucker! Last night she had given herself to him – willingly! These were *his* limbs entwined with hers. She had allowed herself to be tricked into actually enjoying it! A fine rage began to simmer within her breast. Fully awake now, she twisted herself out of his embrace, got up and stood barefoot beside the bed.

"Masta. You need t'git up now. You late fer the fields."

Sally deliberately raised her voice as she spoke. Tucker twitched once then reached for her, encountering empty bedclothes.

"Masta!" Sally shouted this time. "I said you late!"

Tucker sat up finally, rubbing the sleep out of his eyes. Groggily, he focused on Sally.

"Why you hollerin' so? Come on back t' bed. I wanna lay wit' cha some more."

He started to grin at her until he realized how directly she was staring into his face. For the first time, he felt terribly exposed. Last night he'd finally revealed how deeply he loved her. Why was she just standing there looking at him?

"I said come on back t' bed."

Sally promptly pulled back the covers and lay flat on her back beside him. Tucker pulled her close. But the atmosphere had changed completely. *She* had changed. Whatever had possessed her last night seemed now to have evaporated. After a moment, he got up and got dressed. Without another word, he left the cabin, letting the door slam behind him.

CHAPTER 17

$\mathcal{I}$n the days that followed, Sally alternated between self-loathing for betraying Lemuel with Tucker and general rage at the circumstances that now severed her from her lover. Worse yet, she began to worry that Tucker might start suspecting her true relationship to Polly if he noticed how much they looked alike when they were together. This fear finally forced Sally to consider severing ties to her daughter as well. All of these realizations sent her into a deep well of misery. Her appetite, never that robust, vanished completely, along with any hope of ever again sleeping through the night.

Mary would bring Polly to the overseer's cabin in the morning, after he'd left for the fields and return to pick up the baby just as the workers' day was ending. Sally spent every moment carrying Polly wrapped in a blanket against her bosom, rather than on her back, the way the other women carried their nursing infants. With her child in this position, she could gaze into Polly's eyes ever so often and stroke her whenever she cried. Knowing how soon a separation was coming only made Sally need to keep her daughter closer than ever.

Finally, one morning, about a week later, Sally met Mary at the door. As the older woman was about to transfer the baby to Sally's arms, Sally hesitated before taking her daughter.

"Please, come set wit me a spell. I gotta ask a favor." Sally's voice shook as she spoke.

Mary immediately came inside. It was clear that the young woman was more than distressed. Lord knows she had enough reasons for worry!

"Sally, what's wrong?" Mary stopped herself from adding *now*. She stepped inside, handing Polly over in one smooth movement. After a moment's hesitation, she took a seat at the table.

Sally sat across from her cradling her daughter in both arms, "I'm a have t' ask you t' git someone t' nurse Polly fer me. I'm afraid t' keep having her come here. Masta Tucker might start t' see how much we favor one another."

"Oh gal! Y' ain't got t' worry bout that! I told Masta Tucker this here babe were a twin born t' one a the womens what just had two babies. One a 'em were born dead but I ain't told nobody bout the dead one. Far as anybody know, there's the right number a babies round here. Besides, Masta Tucker don't never look at the chil'ren anyways. I seen him look away each time I showed him one a yourn after it were born. I told him the mother ain't had enough milk fer two. He ain't ask me no more questions; just took the child I given him."

Sally looked unconvinced. Mary noted how much worry had changed the girl; she'd grown too thin and her dark eyes now dominated her face.

"You gone have t' stop fretting so," the older woman said, rising to leave. You ain't eating enough t' keep up yer milk. At the door, she stopped. "Sally, don't give up. Things gone git better, I know. Just give it time."

That evening Tucker came home after Mary had taken Polly back to the quarters. Sally had begun dreading his return more each day. He was once again going to expect a recreation of that one night with her and she'd made up her mind that she couldn't do it again. She had, therefore, gathered all the dirty clothing she could find and was busily sorting through the overseer's shirts, trousers and hose just as he was entering.

"Gal!" he exclaimed, surveying the mounds surrounding her, "What the hell you doin?"

"These clothes ain't been washed in a while. Thought I'd git em ready fer tomorrow. Washing em gone take all day as it is. Yer supper's ready. Lemme clear ya a space here on the table."

Sally hurriedly swept aside a load of clothing, set out a plate and began loading it with food. She never looked at Tucker and managed to stay just out of arms reach.

"Sally. Stop." Tucker spoke almost gently. "You ain't ate nothing today, I betcha. Ya gittin skinny. Gitcha a plate an set. I ain't gone touch ya."

She stood still for a moment, then did as she was told. Sitting across from him, she stared down at the boiled potatoes on her plate, fighting the urge to vomit. Finally, she forced herself to take a single bite.

"Sally. Somethin's wrong. I kin tell. Somebody done something t' ya, ya need t' tell me what it is. Ya ain't been right since – since I don't know when. Gal, ya got t' know how much I care about cha. I love ya. Guess ya already figgerd that out way 'fore I ever said it."

Sally stared into her plate. The silence stretched out between them. What could she say? That she didn't want his love, had never asked him to take her in the first place, that she wished he'd never laid eyes on her? She raised her head at last.

"Masta. Ain't nothing wrong. Ain't nobody done nothing to me neither."

CHAPTER 18

Soon it was winter again. By mid-January, the fields and roads were choked with snow hardened into packed ice. Workers crowded into barns and sheds for warmth as soon as their outside chores were done. Inside these close quarters, rumors spread like disease. Mostly, the men whispered about the presumed "rape" of the overseer's woman. Who would've had the nerve to do it? (Every man was secretly jealous of the perpetrator.)

Lemuel overheard two men talking in one of the barns while he was baling hay. At first he paid no attention since neither man was using any names. But, gradually he began to realize they were talking about Sally.

"Heard Masta Tucker still lookin out fer the nigger what touched his woman."

"Ain't nobody told who it is?"

"Don't nobody seem t' know."

"If'n anybody do, it be Peter. He know everything go on round here."

Lemuel hurled his pitchfork into the half-baled hay and stormed out of the barn. Immersed in his misery, he hadn't been spending time with any of the others. In fact, he truly hadn't spoken a word to anyone other than Mary in months.

A fresh storm was brewing and flakes had started to swirl. The sudden shock of cold barely caused a shiver, so intent was he on

finding – and confronting Peter. What story had the man con-
cocted now? What lies was he spreading about Sally?

Peter was standing just outside one of the sheds that stored
the barley used for livestock feed. As soon as Lemuel caught sight
of him, he charged the man, caught him in his midsection and
knocked him to the ground. Without a word, he began pounding
on Peter. Lemuel had the strength of youth and rage but Peter,
even though surprised, had the advantage of a clear head. He easily rolled out of Lemuel's grasp and scrambled to his feet.

"Boy! What got into you, attackin me like that! You gone
daft?"

"What you sayin bout Sally?" Lemuel gasped, getting to his
feet. "You spreadin tales bout how she got raped! You know that
ain't true! Why you trying to stir up more trouble?"

Peter looked at him and said, "Question is why you even
know her name? Don't nobody know the overseer woman's name
but Masta Tucker – an Mary. Mary ain't had no cause t' be telling
you bout that woman, did she?" Peter's eyes narrowed. "So, how
you come t' know it?"

Suddenly, Lemuel realized how Peter had tricked him. He
mentally kicked himself for being so stupid. For the life of him,
he could not think of a plausible lie, so he blurted out the truth.

"Sally an me, we knowed each other from chil'ren. We come
on this place together. I seen Masta Tucker take her on that first
day."

Peter rubbed his jaw, studying the young man steadily.
Suddenly, Lemuel could feel the cold; he fought the urge to shiver.
How much did this man actually know? Lemuel wished to God
he'd been born smarter. He tried to calm down and stop shaking.

"Guess I know why y' wasn't too interested in m' daughter,
seein as how y' knowed this Sally so well." Peter's voice betrayed
just the slightest hint of bitterness. "As to me spreadin tales like

you say, that weren't me. Niggers just making up stories cause they don't know no better."

Lemuel, now completely flustered, took a step back; his foot landed on a slick patch of iced-over snow and he fell solidly on his behind. Embarrassed as well as frightened, he struggled to get up, only to slip again on that same patch. When he finally regained his footing, he mumbled an apology and turned to go.

"Wait a minute." Peter's calm voice stopped him in his tracks. "Think we got a bit more t' talk about."

Lemuel turned slowly to face the man. Somehow, he knew that, whatever Peter was about to say, he would have to go along with.

"Think y' aught t' start takin yer evening meals wit me an m' daughter from now on. Give you two a chance t' git t' know one 'nother. I'm a let Mary know an git yer rations transferred over t' me. That be alright wit you, won't it?"

Lemuel nodded miserably. "Anything else, Mista Peter?"

"Just be there tonight."Abruptly, Peter about faced and went into the shed, leaving the young man standing in the now thickly falling snow.

For over six years, Lemuel realized, he'd been completely at the mercy of the fates that had brought him and Sally to this place. Neither of them had done anything other than try to love one another. And perhaps they could have gone on meeting in secret. But sooner or later, someone would have found out. Anyone else would have run to Master Tucker with the news, anxious to curry any crumbs of favor he could. But it was Peter – Peter who had the plans and designs on him.

For the rest of the afternoon, Lemuel turned the situation over in his mind. He could think more clearly now and he examined the thing from all sides. On its face, Peter held the complete advantage. Although he'd never mentioned a baby, Lemuel suspected that Peter either knew about Polly for sure or had his strong suspicions. He would use keeping the affair and the infant a secret as leverage over Lemuel.

This meant Lemuel had no choice when it came to Peter's daughter, whether he liked her or not. What if the girl didn't fancy him? Lemuel almost laughed aloud at the thought. Peter manipulated everyone – why not his own daughter! The man would have convinced the girl to accept anyone he brought to her.

Somehow, Lemuel thought, I got t' stop this. It ain't fair t' the girl an it'll hurt Sally when she find out. But, he still couldn't figure out how to protect their daughter. Then his mind went back to the gossip. What if he kept the story going by letting slip the possibility that it was *he* who was the rapist? Only Peter would know the truth and he'd have to keep quiet, else everyone would wonder why he didn't tell on Lemuel himself.

As soon as he'd heard the horn, Lemuel ran directly to Mary's shack. He suddenly needed to see Polly; somehow, he couldn't shake the feeling that he might not be able to safely visit his daughter again. Mary was outside, talking with a group of parents who were there to pick up their children. Lemuel slipped past the group unnoticed. Once inside, he scanned the now-bundled up babies and toddlers, looking for his own. A small fair-skinned girl sat on the floor by the fireplace with Polly on her lap. The baby was able to sit up almost steadily by now. Lemuel immediately recognized the girl. The smile that spread across his face was almost a reflex.

"I remember you. See y' gotcha a new job now."

"Aint Mary lettin me help her take care a the littlest chil'ren. An I'm good at it too! See?"

Sally's eldest daughter held up the baby. "Wanna hold her? She a real good babe. Don't hardly never cry. Aint Mary take her up to Masta Tucker house fer her feedings, cause, cause… I don't rightly know why."

Lemuel realized Mary and Sally had worked out an arrangement that would allow Sally to nurse Polly during the day without arousing the overseer's suspicions. Thinking about Sally brought up the almost constant ache that sat in his chest just beneath his heart. At the same time, Lemuel felt deeply proud of her resourcefulness.

He squatted and took Polly from little Mary's outstretched arms. The baby regarded him with the same mild, wide-eyed curiosity that she did everyone else. She was used to being in so many different arms that she never showed a preference for Lemuel's. He wondered whether she was the same way with her mother; he hoped not. For a few precious moments, he held his baby close while Mary stared up at him with a decidedly puzzled expression.

"Why you holdin her like that? You must like her special. That it?"

"Yeah," Lemuel sighed, setting Polly down on the little girl's lap, "Guess I do. Wisht she was mine t' keep. You doing a good job takin care a her, though, like y' say." He slipped out as unnoticed as he'd entered.

It was well after dark when Lemuel finally reached Peter's cabin. Peter was already at the table eating. His daughter Lucy stood by the fireplace, her back to the door, ladling soup into two bowls set on the hearth. Lemuel stopped in the open doorway.

"Sorry I'm a bit late." He decided not to offer an explanation.

Peter put down his spoon and turned slightly. "We just gittin started. Come on in. Lucy," Peter called out to his daughter over his shoulder, "set Lemuel a place."

Lucy brought the bowls to the table, setting one down across from her father's. She gestured toward the spot, then took a seat at the other end. She smiled slightly in Lemuel's direction before beginning to eat. Lemuel hesitated before taking the seat offered and the meal passed in awkward silence. As soon as he'd finished, Peter rose, put on a second shirt and wrapped his neck with a length of woolen fabric. Taking up his pipe, he announced that he'd "be back directly." Then he stepped outside, closing the door behind him.

Lucy spoke up for the first time. "Well, I see my father ain't lost no time gittin you t' come fer supper. He just told me this morning somebody 'might' be stoppin by." She had that same slightly rueful smile.

"Yeah. He told me bout the same time."

Lucy gave Lemuel a level stare. "Somethin y' need t' know right now. Whatever my father told you, I ain't interested in no man just yet. Takin care a him is more 'n enough extra work fer me, along wit the fields. Another man just be twice as much. I love Pa, I do – but, no, I don't want no man. Not right now."

Lemuel breathed a sigh of relief. The girl was much more sensible and practical than he'd expected. Now, he could allow himself to actually look at her. Lucy must have resembled her mother because she looked nothing like Peter. Her face possessed the kind of mature bone structure that wasn't particularly attractive in a young girl but would become quite handsome, once she got older. And she was tall, almost as tall as he was. Yes, he did like her. And no, there was no way he was going to court her. In fact, he decided to plant the seeds of his deception right here, within Peter's own home.

"Yer father do think I'd make y' a good husband but you right bout not wantin t' be wit me. Yer father don't really know what kind a man I am. I done a real bad thing."

"What cha done?"

"Best you didn't know."

Lucy looked decidedly troubled. Lemuel hastened to add, "Listen. I'm sorry I said anything t' upset cha. Just didn't want cha t' think I'm a good man when I ain't. Yer father made it so I gotta come here fer my meal every day but you don't have t' talk t' me if'n you don't wanna."

Instead of answering him, Lucy studied Lemuel silently for several minutes. When she finally spoke, it was with some hesitancy. "I think I'm a let you decide fer yerself if'n y' wanna say anything t' my father, cause I ain't gone say nothin. But, I ain't sure if 'n you really all that bad, seein as how you warned me off. You welcome t' come fer meals long as y' want. Talk or don't. It's up t' you."

The door opened and Peter entered, ushering in a blast of cold air and the faint aroma of tobacco. As he shed his extra clothing, he asked, "You two git acquainted?"

Lemuel answered, "Yessir." He made ready to leave.

Lucy had her back to both men as she busily cleaned up dishes and cooking utensils. She said nothing more.

CHAPTER 19

*N*ow that Lemuel and Lucy had been brought into each other's proximity, Peter felt confident his plans were falling into place. The only problem remaining was Tucker. For some reason, the overseer couldn't seem to get the idea out of his head that Sally had been assaulted and he kept pestering Peter to bring him the culprit.

Peter had tried to get Tucker to reveal what Sally might have said to make him so suspicious but, in truth, Peter, had always found talking to the overseer a challenge. How difficult it was to disguise his true feelings while appearing to actually care about whatever Tucker was saying.

In the end, when it came to Sally's supposed rape, no matter how solicitously Peter tried for an explanation, all he could get from the man was, "I knows my woman an that's what happened t' her."

So, Peter tried to think of a different approach. Perhaps, if the overseer was so obsessed with this attack, only Sally herself, could convince the man that it never happened. But how to get Sally to go along? Peter remembered his one conversation with the young woman – how he'd blackmailed her ruthlessly, how thoroughly beaten she'd looked. What could he say now that would get her to make Tucker believe nothing had happened?

This line of thought was completely unfamiliar to Peter. He'd never considered the nature of Tucker's relationship with Sally as possibly being difficult for the overseer too. Yes, he understood that Sally doubtless hated her owner; that was to be expected. But apparently in Tucker's case, the man had actually come to care for his woman. Peter remembered how his wife Lucy had told him that a woman could tell if a man truly loved her. Lucy had said that's why she'd married him right away when he'd asked her, seemingly out of the blue. Now he wondered whether Sally knew how the overseer felt about her – and if she did, whether she cared.

A few days after Lemuel had begun his evening visits, Peter was leading a work crew to one of the distant barns to do repairs when he overheard a conversation.

"They's word goin' round bout the nigger what touched Masta Tucker woman."

"What they sayin?"

"Sayin it be Lemuel!"

"Him? That nigger don't say two words t' nobody! He quiet as a field mouse, that one! How he git up the nerve t' do somethin like that?"

"It be them quiet ones y' gotta watch!"

Peter stopped so abruptly that the two men speaking bumped into him. He whirled around and fixed them both with a glare so intense that they dropped their eyes and stared fixedly at the ground.

"What you niggers talkin bout?" Peter's voice rose, even though he tried to keep it low. "You don't even know what day it is an you talking bout 'they say!' You ain't know nothin bout nothin happened t' the ovaseer woman! Y' need to keep y' lyin mouths shut!"

Peter knew he'd frightened these two into silence, but only in his presence. Besides, they were only repeating a story they'd heard somewhere else. Why in the world would someone have started this rumor! With an actual name out there, it would be only a matter of time before Tucker got wind of it. And of course he would come straight to Peter for confirmation. The situation had now become too dangerous to wait out. Peter had to find the source of the story and try to put an end to it.

The two men had fallen back into the group that was still tramping along behind Peter. He watched everyone get started on the repairs, then went to find those two. They were working together, one holding a board in place while the other prepared to drive in the nails. Neither man noticed when Peter came and stood behind them. They both jumped when he spoke up and the man holding the board dropped it on his own foot.

"Who told you niggers it were Lemuel?" This time, Peter kept his voice low and gentle. Even so, he had to repeat the question, since the two men simply stared at him open-mouthed. "I said, where you hear it were Lemuel?"

"Wha-why somebody say the boy confessed it hisself," the man holding the nails stammered.

"An who was it sayin?" Peter's voice had now dropped into a deadly monotone.

By now the poor man was actually shaking. "It were Quash what said it. Said Lemuel told him hisself."

Peter took a step back. Completely stunned, he turned, walked a few steps, stopped and came back to the two.

"You gonna have t' stop talkin bout this. I'm a look into it fer myself. Don't wanna hear no more a this talk from nobody else neither! Y' hear? Do an I'm a come lookin fer the two a you!"

That same evening, after Peter, Lucy and Lemuel had finished supper, instead of taking up his pipe, Peter asked Lemuel to join him in a walk. Both men bundled up as best they could and set out on the path leading away from the quarters. For the first time in a week there was no nighttime snowstorm. However, the drifts were too deep to go very far.

Peter faced Lemuel squarely.

"Boy. What 'cha tryin t' do? Why you started that lie bout you an Sally?"

Instead of answering, Lemuel turned to gaze at the clustered shacks. He was silent for so long that Peter was about to repeat the question.

"Y' know, Mista Peter. It seem t' me like you be tryin to run everybody round here. First day here, after Masta Tucker taken Sally, all y' done was t' tell us new niggers t' move on quick. Been like that ever since. Seem t' me like y' got enough say over all a us niggers. Y' aughtn't a had t' hurt me an Sally special. We wasn't doin nothing t' you. Yeah, I was wit Sally. Like I told ya, she were my gal long fore we got here. I wasn't gone make her just be wit the ovaseer if'n she wanted t' be wit me." Lemuel turned back to face Peter. "I done decided that y' daughter don't deserve a man what don't love her. I loves Sally. I'm a go t' my grave lovin her. I think, maybe, y' might understand something bout that kind a love."

Peter said nothing for many minutes as they stood silently facing one another. An errant gust of wind stirred up a whirling snow devil, sparkling tiny jewels in the moonlight. Finally, he spoke up. "Listen son, what' cha done, startin that story, even if'n it true, it ain't gone end good fer you nor yer gal. Masta Tucker been hearin rumors fer a while now. An he been after me t' find out who it were. I'm a have t' tell him somethin, sometime. If' n I say it were you, you gone git the whipping a yer life, I kin tell ya. Betcha y' ain't never been whipped. Y' ain't that kind a hard-headed nigger what git whipped. An y' ain't stupid nor lazy neither. I think y' needs t' see what kin happen t' ya. Foller me."

Peter led the way through deep drifts to the nearest barn, the one that housed the horses and wagons. He pushed the door open. Just inside he used his flint to light a lantern hung from one of the lower rafters. Lemuel joined him in the center of the flickering yellow circle.

"Want' cha t' study it up close," Peter said, peeling off layers of clothing. He pulled his long shirt out of his trousers, turned away and raised it. His entire back was a map in high relief; wreathed, gashed and cratered. Huge ridges of skin had grown up, intersecting deep valleys.

"The ovaseer what done this, he were before Masta Tucker. All I done was t' run away. Run a few times, what I done. Slave kin git his foot cut fer that so I' s lucky, I guess. Still, this whipping most killed me. Lucy, m' wife, she the one save me. Ain't nobody round here t' save you. An Masta Tucker ain't as good wit the whip."

Lemuel stared at Peter's ruined back. It was true that he'd never really thought about the consequences of his confession. For the first time he felt a touch of fear. But, it was too late to reverse course now.

"Mista Peter, sir. I kin see what' cha sayin it be true. An yeah, I ain't never been whipped. But things done gone too far now. If' n it be like y' say, y' gone have t' tell Masta Tucker it were me. An I'm a have t' take m' punishment."

"What about' cha gal? How Sally gone feel, knowin what' cha done? Y' should a thought bout her 'fore y' done anything," Peter said, tucking his shirt into his trousers and putting the layers of clothing back on. "We gone have t' try an keep this thing quiet fer as long as possible. Think y' both got somebody else t' consider here."

Both men fell silent – the unseen specter of Polly floated between them. Lemuel started to shiver, suddenly acutely aware of the cold. Was it possible that Peter had somehow found out about his and Sally's baby? Lemuel didn't want to trap himself yet again.

"Who else we got t' consider?"

Instead of answering him directly, Peter said, "All I'm sayin is t' let me quiet this thing down. I done told the niggers what was spreadin the tale what I'd do t' em if'n I heard another word. Let's just see if'n they's as scared a me as they is a Masta Tucker."

Lemuel's eyes narrowed. He studied Peter's face, searching for clues to the deeper meaning of the man's words.

"So, you think y' can stop all the talk? For real?"

Lemuel wasn't at all convinced, either that no worker would dare going to Master Tucker, or that Peter had given up his original plans for his daughter. But for now, at least, Lemuel decided to let Peter have his way. After all, Lucy had made her own wishes clear, so there was no need to rush into anything.

"Just don't cha say nothin else t' nobody." Peter said as he opened the barn door. "I'm a have a talk wit Quash an git him t' shut up about it."

Peter extinguished the lantern and both men headed back to the shack.

CHAPTER 20

*J*anuary went by; then February. For many years now – almost for as long as anybody could remember, a pattern of deeply cold winter months had seemed permanently stamped upon the whole northeast. It had become more and more difficult for the teamsters moving goods between the farms and cities of the colony to complete their deliveries. Often, from December through March, they would make no visits to the Van Driessen farms at all.

Fortunately, the farms were fairly self-sufficient. The largest hogs would be butchered and the meat smoked for storage, with the best parts set aside. What was left over would become part of the farm's rations. If produce could not be shipped, at least the overseer and workers would not starve. Women spent their days spinning flax and weaving cloth. And the ever-abundant hay made good insulation; it was used liberally – to chink openings in slaves' cabin walls, to fill their mattress ticking and to line their worn-out shoes. During the long dark evenings, men and women used the extra hours to make such repairs to their homes, mend their threadbare clothing and to generally try to keep themselves as warm as possible.

Forced to stay inside Tucker's cabin, Sally filled her days with an almost unceasing round of chores. She cleaned every piece of crockery and every cooking utensil, swept the hearth clear of soot and laid in fresh wood. Then she tackled the assortment of tools that Tucker had never bothered to organize. She polished blades and shovels, cleaned years of dirt off spade handles.

When she'd finished with the tools, she set about hanging them on nails, grouped by use: Tucker's two spades side-by-side with his shovel; his many different-sized hobbles beside the reins he used on his horse. But it was the collection of whips that stopped her. Sally had never noticed them before. They lay semi-hidden in a corner behind the door: a coiled bullwhip; two identical smaller whips and one particularly fierce-looking thing with a heavy handle and plaited straps, sharp bits of metal attached to every one. She took up each whip, gauged its size and weight, then drove a nail into the wall beside the door and hung it up, neatly coiled.

Indeed, her self-imposed chores had never before included a thorough cleaning of the cabin at all. Tucker only cared about his food and her being available whenever he wanted sex. And she had always paid the same amount of attention to the place that the overseer did. Now, however, Sally truly needed to keep busy trying to fill her empty days and wear herself out by nightfall so she'd be able to sleep, even if only for a few hours.

A large part of the emptiness, besides the endless longing for Lemuel, was because she no longer had milk for Polly. Sally had tried, without success to keep up her supply but, for the first time, her body failed her. She'd simply lost too much weight. Frightened that her baby might be suffering, Sally finally begged Mary to find a wet nurse.

"I think Polly might be ready t' try a cup." Mary had replied gently. "She real sturdy an she wanna be like the older ones, so she probably take t' it pretty quick. Think y' better let me do it, though. Seein her ma'am only keep her askin fer the tit."

Sally knew what Mary meant; this was to be their final separation. She kissed Polly and held her so tight that, after a time, the baby began to squirm. Mary took the child from Sally's arms, bundled her up and headed back to the quarters. Sally stood shivering outside, watching them until the copse of trees cut off her view. She then went back inside and closed the door.

When Tucker returned that evening, he found Sally sitting amidst a huge mound of his clothing, furiously sorting through the shirts and trousers. She didn't even look up as he entered.

"What' cha doin now," he asked irritably. "Gittin ready t' wash again? Think y' done washed everything I own at least twice already!"

Sally seemed not to notice his annoyance. She answered in the monotone that seemed to have now become her normal tone of voice.

"Lot a these clothes is still good. Just need t' be let out so's they can be worn. I'm a work on 'em tomorrow. Just set a bit an I'll git yer supper directly."

Tucker watched her fold each piece before heading over to the hearth. He came up behind her as she was about to spoon hot stew into his bowl. Slipping both arms around her waist, he leaned down and kissed the back of her neck. Sally stiffened and dropped the heavy ladle back into the kettle, splashing the stew all over her hands. She stood, seemingly frozen, staring silently as the skin began to blister. Tucker, at once horrified and galvanized, grabbed up the water pitcher and poured the contents over her burns.

"Sally!" he shouted, "Gal! You gone daft? Ain't cha seen what' cha was doin? How come you jumped like that? Cause I touched ya? That it? I cain't touch ya now without you jumpin like I's some kinda snake?" Tucker's voice had kept rising until now he was nearly screaming.

Sally whirled around and faced the overseer squarely.

"You hadn't aughta been sneakin up behind me! That's what! You scared me! How I know what' cha was gone do?" She was suddenly shouting too. "Think I got eyes in the back a' my head so's I kin see what' cha doing behind me?"

She watched Tucker's face redden, veins suddenly swollen in his neck and forehead. His right hand twitched almost convulsively. She steadied herself, ready for the blow that, surely, had to come this time. Yes, she did want him to hit her – hit her hard enough to kill her!

Instead, he pulled her against him; lifting her off the floor, he held her tight. She could feel his heart beating and somehow that connected with the throbbing pain in both hands. It all became strangely pleasurable – the pulsing against her breast, her hands' searing heat. It was almost as satisfying as a beating. She wrapped both arms around his neck.

"If' n ya wanna, y' kin take me t' bed, now," she said flatly.

"Lemme take care a yer hands first."

"No!" she snapped, "Bed now or not at all!"

In the days that followed, Sally and Tucker alternated between arguments and stony silences. Clearly, he was too much in love to exercise any kind of discipline over her and she knew it. Gradually, she became the one who initiated both the fights and the silences. And she began to control their lovemaking, as well. Not that she could actually refuse him, of course; Tucker still took her whenever he wanted. What Sally now did was to withhold any kind of active participation, especially after an argument. She would simply lie there silently while he worked as hard as he could to bring forth some sort of reaction from her. Usually he would finish alone. Then, frustrated and exhausted, he'd roll over and go to sleep. She would simply lie awake, waiting for daybreak.

Sally knew Tucker had no idea why she would respond to him only every few times. Actually, she really never wanted to; it was just that, every now and again, she couldn't help herself. It was as though his love was an actual force, endlessly pushing against her will to resist him. And it did seem that he'd begun to learn how to arouse her, at least occasionally. After one of those rare occasions, instead of falling asleep, Tucker rested on both elbows and gazed down at her for many moments.

"Sally," he whispered, "gal, you still awake?"

She slowly opened her eyes.

"Seem t' me like it bout time you should be gittin wit child. Y' ain't nursin nobody's babe an – an…." He started to stammer, then fell silent.

Sally turned her face away. His gaze had become so intense that she could feel it, even in the darkness. She hadn't even thought about getting pregnant again but, of course, it was bound to happen – and probably soon.

"What I'm sayin is, this time it'll be different. Y' won't lose this 'un. I'll see t' it. I'm a take good care a ya this time. You'll see." He kissed her, and then promptly lay on his side, apparently satisfied that he'd finally made her happy.

Now she had something else to dread.

CHAPTER 21

*B*y the time March had melted into April, the worst of the storms seemed finally over. There were days filled with cold rain and gusty winds that finally gave way to milder sunny weather. As April drew to a close, spring finally began in earnest. Everyone set about preparing for the first grain harvest. Spring wheat had to be planted by May to be ready for harvest in mid-August. Barley, which ripened first, could be put in along with the wheat. Corn, too, had to be sown now, since that crop took so much longer to ripen. Each day's work began well before sunrise and only ended when there was absolutely no daylight left.

A gang of slaves was moving boulders left in one of the fields after the last snow melt. Working in teams, one man would dislodge a boulder while the other upended a wheelbarrow and wedged it underneath. Then both men would wrestle with the load, one straining to get the boulder into the barrow, the other fighting to steady the thing. Once they'd gotten their burden secured, there'd be the chore of moving it out of the field without having the barrow tip over causing them to have to repeat the whole task.

Tucker had chosen to supervise this field to make sure the workers actually cleared it completely – a single forgotten boulder could break a ploughshare and set the planting back for weeks. Besides, observing the workers so closely gave him more of an

opportunity to eavesdrop. It did seem, these days, like the workers had gotten unusually quiet in their conversations, even when
he didn't appear to be looking in their direction. And, of course,
this made him all the more suspicious. Peter had never gotten
back to him with the name of Sally's attacker. By now, Tucker was
certain Peter knew who it was and had decided not to tell him.

Quash was a simple man, vain and fond of talk – especially
gossip, but essentially lacking in guile. He'd never intended to
create havoc when he'd repeated the story Lemuel had told him in
confidence. He just couldn't help himself. During the month or
so he'd spent repeating, and even embellishing Lemuel's confession, he'd been the center of attention. By the time Peter got to
him, the story had spread to almost every one of the slaves. Only
Mary hadn't heard, since everyone knew what a low opinion she
held for gossip and those who spread it.

Peter made sure to get Quash alone. The man had a wife and
two fairly young children, the last of eight and the only ones to
have survived. Late one evening, Peter made a visit to the shack
Quash and his family shared with another family of equal size.
Peter greeted everyone, then asked Quash to join him outside for
a smoke.

The two men walked a short ways down the dirt path. Quash
had no pipe – didn't even smoke, in fact, but he was much too
afraid of Peter to refuse the invitation. Peter took his time lighting
up and drawing on the clay stem until the embers glowed. Then
he blew a perfect circle of smoke before speaking.

"Want 'cha t' understand me, so I'm a say this so's y' kin,"
Peter began. Then he switched into Dutch, "Luistert goed me!
Spreekt nog één woord van Lemuel en Meester Tuckers meid
en ik vermoord je!" ("Hear me good! Say one word more about
Lemuel and Master Tucker's wench and I will kill you!")

The man's mouth fell open. Unable to muster any kind of a response, he could only stand there staring as Peter took another draw on his pipe, then turned and casually walked off.

Peter's first master, Samuel Gerritson, was a descendent of one of the earliest Dutch emigrant families into the colony of Rensselearwyck, a huge land grant that included areas surrounding the city of Albany and extending both east and west of the Hudson River. Samuel was, in fact, directly descended from Wolfert Gerritson, the colony's first overseer, which meant that he'd inherited a large portion of the Gerritson family's fortune. Peter became his personal servant when they were both still in their teens. Samuel, unfortunately, had neither the intellect to manage his affairs nor the inclination to hire competent men to do the work for him. By the time he reached manhood, Samuel had wasted most of his inheritance and was deeply in debt. In fact, all that was left in his name was his house, a few acres and several slaves, including Peter.

Samuel needed to sell off the slaves in order to retire the balance of his debts. Because Peter was the youngest and healthiest, he should have been able to fetch a price that equaled the value of Samuel's entire holdings, had the man been shrewd enough to demand it. Unfortunately, Samuel did not. Instead, he sold Peter for 100 guilders to a slave merchant who happened to stop by the property one day offering to "take any extra merchandise ya got."

Peter's next master was a farmer trying to scratch out a living on his fifteen acres just west of the Hudson River. The man, whose name was Johannas deGroot, had been a tenant farmer for about eight years on land belonging to the van Rensselaer estate. When it became clear that this farm wasn't ever going to produce profitably, the absentee owner, Stephen van Rensselaer II allowed deGroot to purchase the land. At that point, the farmer decided to buy one slave. He needed a strong back to help with the work.

So, when he encountered the itinerate merchant and his wagon-full of slaves on the road near his farm, deGroot carefully looked over the entire gang. Searching out the strongest-looking man, who happened to be Peter, deGroot began negotiations. The slave merchant knew the actual value of his stock much better than Peter's former master had and he set a price that would have cost deGroot dearly. After haggling for nearly an hour, the two men finally settled on a price that was still too high for deGroot. In the end, however, the farmer paid it, deciding he would just need to work this man that much harder to make back his costs. And so, Peter got his first taste of the fields.

On the next farm over, that owner was having a much easier time making a living. His land was crisscrossed with several small streams, which provided enough natural irrigation for his crops to come in healthy and lush each season. This man kept a family of slaves to help him tend his fields: a father, two grown sons and a sixteen-year-old daughter who worked outside with the rest of her family.

One day, while on an errand for deGroot, Peter passed by the neighbor's field where the girl was cutting rye and stopped to watch her. He had never before been this close to a young black woman; all the slaves in Gerritson's household had been much older and he was never allowed to mingle with the field hands. The brilliant slant of an afternoon sun rendered her figure in moving silhouette, one strong bare arm swinging her scythe, the other gathering up the beheaded stalks and depositing them onto the pile at her feet..

The girl, sensing his stare, straightened up, turned in his direction and gave him a wide smile. Now that she had moved out of the direct sunlight, Peter could see her clearly. She boldly dropped her scythe and, with barely a backward glance over her shoulder, came close to the split-rail fence where he was standing. He would later try to explain the mystery of that meeting to Lucy.

"I do swear, fer the life a me, at that moment, I couldn't make out nothin' but a pure angel – a black angel if'n ya can believe that! Couldn't tell ya nothing else bout how she looked nor what she said t' me. Seem like, from that first moment we was gone be together, somehow!"

And they did meet as often as Peter could slip away in the dead of night. They met in the fields, in the neighbor's barn, behind the chicken coop, anyplace they could find that was away from the prying eyes of her owner and her family. Of course the girl got pregnant – and quickly.

When her condition grew so evident that it could no longer be ignored, the girl confessed to her father and named Peter as her lover. Her father took the matter to his master, who was completely sanguine about the entire affair. As Peter told it to Lucy, the girl's owner decided to allow the couple to continue meeting, and to say nothing about it to deGroot, even after the girl turned up with child for a second, and then a third time.

"That man weren't no fool." Peter explained. "He knowed any babe borned t' one 'a his slaves belonged t' him. He were just increasin' his own holdings. But that weren't gone be the case fer me if'n my master was t' find out!" Peter knew that deGroot would be dead set against his slave enriching his neighbor. "So I set out t'try 'n git my master t' buy my gal so's we wouldn't be separated."

deGroot would have none of it. Peter had already cost him the value of one year's harvest and in the three ensuing years, deGroot had barely recouped the full amount. He forbade Peter's continuing the visits. In fact, deGroot confronted his neighbor, who by now could boast that he owned a proven breeder who had already produced three live nigger babes. But deGroot, far from offering to buy the wench, demanded that his neighbor exercise some restraint over her. The neighbor complained that it was Peter who was in need of restraint. After all, his slaves know how to remain on their master's farm; Peter was the one who did all the roaming.

Three years of this, coupled with two more poor harvests in a row finally convinced deGroot to cut his losses and sell Peter. Although the man was a good enough worker, the two of them still couldn't make the farm produce. And deGroot decided that he could no longer stomach a slave who would disobey him so flagrantly. Despite repeated, if ineffectual floggings, Peter had continued to visit the neighbor's wench. So, when a representative of the Reverend Van Driessen happened to be in Albany inquiring about the purchase of some slaves to work his farms, the representative was given deGroot's paper announcement. The man then made the trip to deGroot's farm to negotiate the sale.

Peter learned about his fate when the two men came looking for him behind the barn where he'd been sharpening a plowshare. deGroot simply told him to "jes drop whatever yer doin' an' git in that wagon yonder. I'm done wit'cha!"

Instead of doing as he was told, Peter sprinted for the open field with both men in pursuit. He was only trying to reach the road that separated deGroot's farm from his neighbor's. If he could get within shouting distance, he could yell for his girl to come and bid him farewell.

"I hollered loud as I could an' she come a'runnin'. She were big again, carryin' m' last child, so she couldn't move too good. My master an' that other white man caught up, hog-tied me an' throwed me in the wagon. They couldn't stop me from yellin' that I was gone find my way back one day. That's the reason I kept on runnin'."

As Peter told the tale to Lucy, he would come to realize how futile the entire situation had been at the time. He'd never have been able to get back to the area since he had no clear idea where *back* was. Having never traveled the roads, even in the company of his masters, he might as well have been in a foreign country.

Eventually, the years with Lucy would erase even the girl's name from his memory; yet, even now, Peter could still see her, heavy with child, sobbing by the side of the road as the wagon carried him away forever.

Yes, Peter understood quite well how Lemuel felt about Sally.

When the eavesdropping yielded nothing, Tucker had a revelation. They *all* knew who the perpetrator was! These slaves had decided, together, to protect whoever had raped Sally – and Sally herself was in on it! This meant it was more important to her to keep him from finding and punishing her rapist, even if the man had caused the death of their first owned child! Tucker determined, at that moment, he would catch this man, whip him within an inch of his life and make Sally watch!

The overseer found Peter in the main barn, shoeing one of the horses. Peter stopped working when the man's shadow crossed his shoulder.

"Listen here," Tucker barked, "Want 'cha t' assemble every single slave right now! I got somethin t' say they all need t' hear!"

Peter had been on his knees, prying off the old shoe. He got up and left immediately. Something about the overseer's expression warned him not to ask any questions.

One hour later, everyone had gathered in a clearing at the beginning of the path leading to Tucker's cabin. They all milled around uneasily; these kinds of assemblies only meant one thing – someone was about to be whipped. The entire group turned as

Tucker's horse galloped into sight along the main road. He dismounted and charged past them, heading toward his cabin.

Sally was nowhere to be seen. Tucker's eyes swept the cabin walls and floor. She had organized his tools so well that now he could barely find anything. Her logic of putting like items together meant that nothing was where it had always been before – which had been in the last place he'd dropped it.

He finally found the whips neatly coiled on individual nails beside the door. He was about to grab the bull whip, but, instead his hand lingered over the cat-o-nine-tails. A voice in his head sounding exactly like old Van Roop's said, *Don't!* And he did hesitate for only a second before taking the thing off its nail. Telling himself that this will scare the truth out of them faster, he ran out, leaving the door wide open.

"All a ya niggers listen real good!" Tucker shouted, "One a ya taken liberties wit m' woman an I know somebody know who it were done it." He strode into the midst of the workers and continued, "I'm a give the coward just one last chance t' confess 'fore I start into whippin' every goddamn one a ya!"

Peter stepped forward. "Masta Tucker. Sir. I done told ya ain't nobody done such a thing. If'n it'd happened, don't' cha think ya gal would've told ya so, Sir?"

Tucker turned on Peter. "Nigger!" he bellowed, "You the one been lyin' t' me the whole time! You know'd who done it all along an wouldn't say nothin'. I'm a start wit you!"

Suddenly, before Peter could say another word, Lemuel spoke up. "It were me, Masta Tucker." Although Lemuel's voice was firm and he looked Tucker straight in the eye, he could feel his whole insides trembling. He fought to keep from shaking visibly.

"You touched m' woman? You?" Tucker stared incredulously. Why this nigger was one of the best workers on the place. Had never given a moment's worth of trouble neither.

"I done it, Masta. It weren't nobody's fault but mine. I seen y' woman out washin' clothes an – an I just done it. If'n she ain't wanna tell. I guess it were cause she just wanna forget about it."

Peter whirled round to face Lemuel – effectively turning his back on the overseer. For the moment he forgot about Tucker. The boy had clearly lost his mind! Hadn't he agreed to let Peter take care of everything?

"Nigger," he hissed at Lemuel, "You need t' shut up!"

"No!" Lemuel shouted this time, "I done it! I ain't gone let nobody else take the blame fer what I done!" He stepped around Peter and stared Tucker down. "I'm ready fer anything you gone do!" A curious calm settled over him, steadying the trembling.

The overseer's face, already flushed, grew blood red. This man was actually taunting him—daring him to mete out the punishment! A blinding rage filled Tucker's heart. He screamed at Peter to "tie this nigger t' that tree up yonder an' back up out the way!" Peter didn't move immediately, so Tucker shoved him aside and ordered two others to the task.

The men carried Lemuel to a sturdy elm not far from Tucker's cabin, stripped off his shirt, wrapped his arms around the trunk and tied his wrists together with a length of stout rope.

Uncoiling the cat 'o nine-tails, Tucker drew back and sent the whip curling into Lemuel's body. One of the separate leather straps caught Lemuel across the right cheek, cutting into the skin just below his eye. He stiffened against the blow, his jaw set, teeth bared, eyes squeezed shut. When Tucker sent the next one sizzling, Lemuel took that as well. The crowd sent up a single, horrified gasp.

Sally had been out back drawing water when Tucker entered the cabin and left with the whip. She could just make out that there was some sort of commotion going on down the road, but thought nothing of it until she got to the door, which she knew she'd closed to keep out the flies. Now it stood wide open. Stepping across the sill, she instinctively looked at the row of whips and dropped the bucket. As water spread around her feet, she backed out of the cabin.

Outside, she turned herself round in a complete circle, then flew down the road toward the noise. She reached the clearing just as Tucker was about to deliver the third blow. With that crack of the whip, Sally uttered an involuntary scream—sharp, then strangled at the end, as though she'd suddenly inhaled.

"Stop!" she cried out. "Stop! Don't hit him no more! Please, don't hit him no more!" She tried to run past Tucker to reach Lemuel but the overseer caught her by the wrist. With his free hand, he held her in a grip that truly would have hurt, had she been aware of the pain.

"So, ya wasn't never gone tell me, was ya? Well I found out anyways! Now I'm a show ya what! This nigger gone pay fer what he done! An' you gone watch the whole thing!" He released her wrist and addressed the rest of the workers. "All a ya niggers gone watch! An not one a ya better move a whit, else it'll be your turn next!"

By now, Tucker had gotten some control of himself. This was a familiar part of his job. He even liked administering a good whipping. Done properly, it left stripes that healed clean. The facial cut had been a mistake—sloppy work with an unfamiliar instrument that might have cost Lemuel an eye. But Tucker believed he could lay well-placed lashes that would shortly produce just enough screaming, at which point he would know the lesson had been learnt. He went back to work. This whip did seem to take a bit more effort, but he could handle it.

However, something was amiss. Tucker, his rhythm established, had begun to count the strokes in his head. By the fifth stroke, a slave should have been screaming in agony. Lemuel had taken ten so far without uttering so much as a groan.

So, this nigger gon' test me Tucker thought. Taking a slightly wider stance, he anchored his left heel firmly into the dirt. Now he could put more power behind his whipping arm. The lashes whistled as they cut into Lemuel's back, ripping out first pieces, and then whole chunks of flesh.

Gasping, Lemuel fought the agonizing pain that sliced through him with each stroke. He was afraid he'd have to scream very soon. But he knew Sally was standing somewhere nearby; he'd heard her crying out for him. If she had to witness this horror and listen to his screams as well – no! He couldn't bear the thought of her suffering with him!

Somehow, that decision steeled his resolve. The next stroke brought even more searing pain. Tears squeezed out of the corners of both eyes; his nose began to run and he could taste blood where he'd bitten his tongue. He clenched his jaws even more tightly through the next five lashes. And through yet another five. In the middle of five more, he lost consciousness.

Tucker saw the man's body slump against the tree trunk. "Throw some water on him! Wake him up!" He bellowed at Peter, who ran up the path to fetch a bucket and fill it from Tucker's rain barrel. He dumped the entire bucketful over Lemuel's head; the man stirred slightly, but didn't open his eyes.

Lemuel didn't feel the water or the lashes that followed. To his great surprise, he found himself suspended just above the tree. From this vantage point, he could now witness the whole scene. With amazement, he watched his bound body twitching each time the lash tore into his flesh. He could see Tucker, red-faced, screaming incoherently each time the whips snapped.

And, oh, his poor Sally! She was doubled over, clutching herself in pain–but making not a sound! Yes, he'd made the right decision. Now it no longer mattered how long Tucker whipped him – he would *never* utter a single scream! And then, he no longer had any sense of the clearing, the gathered workers, Tucker, even Sally. He could hear a wind rushing all around him, carrying him away into swirling darkness that exploded – suddenly – into light....

For almost an hour Tucker plied the cat-o-nines. At some point, Lemuel's back finally dissolved into a bloody mass of flesh, fat and muscle. His body slid down until he was on his knees, his head resting against one side of the trunk. Tucker shouted for Peter to wake him again.

Peter approached the tree and touched Lemuel; he gently patted his cheek. Then he straightened up. "Masta Tucker, Sir, I cain't wake him up 'cause he dead."

"He ain't dead!" Tucker shrieked hysterically. "Now do like I told ya' an wake him up!"

Peter leaned over and picked up the bucket. He took his time walking back up the path and refilling it. This time, he poured the contents all over Lemuel. Gobs of loosened flesh washed off, creating a red pool around his knees. The bones of his shoulder blades were now visible. Peter very gently placed two fingers against Lemuel throat and then he straightened up.

"What 'cha waitin fer? Git him up!"

"Masta Tucker, Sir. Like I said, he dead. Sir."

Tucker threw down the cat and strode over to the tree. Pushing past Peter, he grabbed a handful of hair and yanked Lemuel's head back. The young man's face was strangely composed, eyes closed, lips slightly parted. He looked like he'd simply fallen asleep. But there was no doubt that he was dead.

Abruptly, Tucker released his grip on Lemuel's hair, stepped back from the body and looked around wildly. All the workers except Peter had vanished, slipped away as soon as they realized that Lemuel wasn't going to cry out, and Tucker wasn't about to stop until he did. Peter, however, still stood his ground, watching the overseer.

Sally! Tucker whirled around, looking for her. She was still in the same spot where she'd been from the moment he'd released her. "Sally!" he shouted, walking hurriedly in her direction, "Listen, gal! I never meant 't kill him! Just t' learn him not t' touch what ain't his'n! Sally?"

She had started moving toward him. When they were nearly abreast, he could see that she hadn't heard one word. She walked right past, as though he wasn't there. When she reached the tree, she sank to the ground beside Lemuel's crumpled body. Reaching out with both hands, she touched the places where the flesh hung in tatters, caressing the open wounds, trying to smooth the flayed skin back into place. She gently moved his head so she could gaze into his face. The corners of Lemuel's mouth were turned up slightly into the beginnings of that smile she so adored. How amazing that he'd died looking so peaceful!

Peter was still standing a short distance away. Sally raised her eyes from Lemuel and fixed him with the coldest stare possible. Speaking very softly, she said, "Cut him loose."

Stepping forward, Peter cut the rope that had bound Lemuel's wrists. He was sure Sally believed it was he who'd told Masta Tucker about her and Lemuel. He would have to let her continue to think he'd betrayed them. Better for her to have him to hate, along with Masta Tucker. Hate would give her something solid to hold on to. Peter turned his thoughts to Lemuel. Watching Sally rocking the young man's body, all Peter could think was, why? Why had Lemuel been so stubborn! All he'd had to do was scream like he was supposed to, and Masta Tucker would've stopped the whipping. After all, Lemuel was still young and healthy. You didn't kill a valuable slave like that!

Tucker watched Sally's open display of love and grief with a growing sense of betrayal. All this time, he'd been telling himself that whoever raped her must've overcome her first. It had never crossed his mind that Sally could have participated willingly. Not when she belonged to him! Not when he loved her so desperately! Now here she was, cradling Lemuel's head as she laid his body on her lap, heedless to the blood soaking her skirts.

Tucker could feel his rage rising.

He'd kill her! Yes! Kill her as dead as her nigger lover!

"Sally! Git up from there!" Tucker shouted. He'd started in the direction of the tree, fully intending to seize her by the throat and choke the life out of her. Just as he reached her, Sally looked up at him, her face as composed as Lemuel's.

She wants me t' do it, Tucker realized suddenly. She thinks she kin get free a me by me killin her.

The thought stopped him in his tracks. He didn't have to do anything more to Sally. Lemuel was dead; now she'd have to be faithful to him. All he had to do was to wait for her to get over being angry. Reaching down, he grasped Sally by the shoulders and pulled her to her feet.

Lemuel's body rolled off her lap and onto the ground face-up. Sally fought viciously against Tucker's grasp, trying to get loose and go back to Lemuel, but Tucker lifted her up and carried her, bucking and kicking, up the path to the cabin.

Once inside, he set her on her feet. Immediately, Sally lunged past him; she almost made it to the door before he was able to grab her wrist. She struggled against his grip, then started hitting at his face, his body, wherever she could land a blow. Tucker took the blows; he caught her free hand by the wrist, just before she went for his eyes. Placing his back against the door so she couldn't bolt again, he held her at arms length as he once more tried to explain what had happened.

"He wasn't suppose t' die Sally. I just didn't know when t' stop cause he didn't never make no noise. Onliest way I know when I'm suppose t' stop a beatin is when a nigger start in t' screamin good an loud."

Sally heard nothing he was saying, only the terrible roaring in her ears. She sprang at Tucker, clawing and growling like some wild thing. When she finally managed to rake at his eyes, he backhanded her, sending her flying into the table.

She stumbled, righted herself and attacked him again, this time spitting in his face. Tucker reacted by delivering a solid closed-fisted blow to her jaw. Sally fell between the table and bench and lay there, momentarily knocked unconscious. After a moment, she came to, sat up and spat out a mouthful of blood.

Getting unsteadily to her feet, she tried again to make it to the door. And again, Tucker grabbed her.

The overseer could feel his heart pumping hard, the hot rage rising again. "What I wanna know," he yelled, "is how ya come t' play me false like ya done? Sally, ya been my woman ever since ya come here."

"I was Lemuel's long fore I come here. We was promise from chil'ren," Sally shouted, twisting against his grip, her voice rising to a scream.

"Well, ya ain't never said nothin bout ya already had a man when I picked ya."

"You 'ain't never ask me did I have one!" Sally shouted back. The anger in her eyes flashed quick and hot. "An' I don't believe it'd a made no difference t' ya if'n I did. You'd a took me anyways." She was wailing by now, her words nearly choked off by her cries.

She was right, of course. Tucker knew, from the first, that Sally had to be his. She was much too beautiful for any nigger to have her. But Lemuel didn't have to die. Tucker would have prevailed upon Mr. Firth to arrange for him to be moved to one of Van Driessen's other farms closer to Albany.

"The thing is," Tucker drew several long breaths, trying to calm himself, "Sally, I still love ya more'n anythin'." She kicked him sharply as he continued, "I do. Cain't help it an Lord knows I tried. So, no, wasn't no way I could ever give ya up." Still holding her at bay, he backed her away from the door. Then, quickly he pulled her into a near frantic embrace, effectively cutting off her breath. He kept on squeezing her tightly until the fight went out of her. Sally didn't resist his clumsy caresses and awkward kisses. Nor did she stop him from removing her blouse and skirt, the blood on them both now dried stiff.

She realized now that she wasn't going to get free of this man and she hadn't been able to save Lemuel either. It no longer mattered what Tucker did to her.

Tucker made love to Sally until he was spent – till his heart quieted down and he could breathe normal. He forgot that there had been no work done that day. He didn't care that the slaves were probably loafing in the quarters. All he cared about was that Sally was finally his alone. Sooner or later, he decided, almost desperately, she would come to understand why he'd lost control. And that killing Lemuel had been an accident.

An accident was how Tucker decided he would report Lemuel's death to Mr. Firth. Even so, when he told the accountant, the man coolly announced that he would still deduct the cost of the dead worker from Tucker's pay. It meant that Tucker would lose over three year's wages. Owners most often made such losses very expensive for their overseers. It kept the men from using up workers who sometimes couldn't be replaced, especially if the farm was already losing money due to a bad harvest.

CHAPTER 22

"Pa, it true what that Lemuel say? He the one taken Masta Tucker woman?"

Lucy had been silent for nearly a week. She and her father had risen each day, mostly worked apart and spent the evening immersed in necessary tasks. Peter had actually been grateful for the absence of talk. One of the things he loved most about Lucy was her ability to know when to keep still—just like her mother.

"You know, Pa, he did say he done a bad thing. That first night he taken supper wit us, that what he say."

"He told you that? You ain't said nothin t' me bout it."

" I decided t' just wait an' see if' n you was ever gone say somethin'. Figured you'd know whatever it was."

When Peter didn't answer for several minutes, Lucy went back to clearing the table of their supper bowls. They'd had a stew of beans and corn – succotash, the Indians called it. Peter had taught her how to make the dish so thick and filling it didn't even need bacon fat for seasoning. The food warmed his stomach and settled his nerves; under his tutelage, Lucy had truly learned how to cook for a man.

"Lemuel weren't no bad man. Him an the ovaseer woman knowed each other fore they come here. Think they was always plannin t' be husband an wife, but Masta Tucker taken the gal soon as she got on the place. Lemuel, well, he never got over her. An, I guess she never got over him neither."

Lucy had stopped working and come to sit down. She now leaned her elbows on the table, fascinated by the story. "Pa, if'n ya knowed he felt that way, how come ya brought him here?"

"Cause I was tryin t' keep all a this from happenin in the first place!" Peter suddenly roused himself and looked sharply at his daughter. "That gal belong t' the ovaseer! Couldn't nobody else have her! Weren't no sense in Lemuel just pinin' over her. Not when there's other good womens around!" Lucy stared blankly at her father. "Yeah, I mean you," he continued, "I ain't gone be round forever. An I just wanna see ya wit a decent man!"

Getting up from the table, she said, "Well, Pa, Lemuel weren't gone be the one." With her back to him, she added, "Think next time, y' might wanna ask me 'bout it first."

Peter, watching his daughter's deft movements, found himself again yearning for his dead wife. Ever since Lemuel's death, he'd been remembering how Lucy had been able to save his life. Although he'd barely been aware of the woman at the time, she'd tended his wounds and endured his awful screams in those first days and nights. Peter had been unable to move on his own. Once Lucy had cleaned his back, he'd had to lie face down on her bed until solid scabs formed. The pain had made rest impossible, yet he'd had to keep still so as not to disturb the healing. Lucy had allowed him to hold on to her whenever he needed to. And, somehow, she would manage to rock her body in such a way that he was finally soothed enough to fall asleep.

It had been the sleep that had aided his physical healing, but it was Lucy, herself, who'd finally quieted his heart. She'd lain beneath him, fully clothed, night after night. Whenever he'd awaken in complete panic, his heart beating at a gallop, his entire body drenched in cold sweat, Lucy would simply rock her hips from side to side, cradling him until the spell passed. Peter wasn't sure when he'd realized it but, by the time he was well enough to stand up unaided, he couldn't bear even the thought of ever having to leave Lucy's bed. Maybe that was the reason the attacks of terror continued. Peter didn't want Lucy to leave him alone, not even to go outside to draw water; he'd follow her around almost constantly. The only time she could get any privacy was when she had to relieve herself.

Late one evening, when Lucy had finished serving them both supper, the door opened suddenly and there stood the youngster Tucker. The lad stepped awkwardly into the room, trying to look as grown as possible, since he'd come to issue an order.

"Masta Van Roop say that there nigger done had enough time t' git well," Tucker announced to Lucy, gesturing in Peter's general direction, "Masta Van Roop expectin' him an you back in the fields come sun up t'morrow." The young man made another clumsy gesture, ducked his head and then backed himself out the door, closing it behind him.

At the sight of Tucker's white face, Peter had started shaking. He'd sat silently through the announcement, trying to conceal the fact that he was trembling. He could feel his heart racing and his palms growing clammy.

"Miz Lucy," he stammered, as soon as the youngster had left, "I know I'm actin like the worst coward ya ever saw! Don't know why, but I just git scared fer no good reason! I weren't like this before!"

Lucy came and sat beside him on the bench. She quietly took up one of his hands. "The kind a whipping you had, well, that's how it leaves mens. Seem like it just take everything outta em. Ya gone feel like this fer a while, but it do go away after a spell. You be better bye an bye."

Peter wasn't really listening to her words; he was suddenly completely focused on the woman herself, every part of her. Lucy had always assumed that she was plain, her features easily inter-changeable with those of any other black woman. Peter, however, was seeing something else entirely, a woman he wanted to – indeed, needed to stay with for the rest of his life. But, how she felt about him, well, Peter had no idea. She had allowed him to share her bed though and that may have put a truly dangerous thought into his head. Actually, it was much more of an impulse, but one so strong he knew he wasn't going to be able to resist it much longer.

Later, in the dead of night, Peter was awakened by the most intense desire he'd ever known. Lucy, sleeping lightly as she always seemed to, felt his heart thumping against her chest and began the rocking motion that had always soothed him. But to-night, Peter's hands moved down her body, caressing her hips, her thighs and, finally pulling up her skirts. In the next movement, he'd pulled down his trousers, entered her and commenced mak-ing love furiously. Lucy didn't move until he'd reached his explo-sive climax, shuddered and finally collapsed on top of her. At that point, she pushed him off, got up and pulled down her skirts. She walked to the bench and sat.

"I see you feelin quite a bit better now. Seem t' me you 'bout ready t' be leavin'," she said, her voice even.

Peter nearly fell off the bed trying to get up and pull up his pants at the same time. "Miz Lucy, please! Fer God sake I ain't mean t' do what I done! I mean, I been wantin' to, but not like that! I love ya is what! I-I need t' marry ya! Please don't send me away! Please let me stay!" His voice broke at the end and tears filled his eyes.

She studied him from where she sat, silently and for several minutes. Peter could feel that awful sense of panic rising in his chest, making his heart hammer sickeningly. At last she spoke, a single word, "yes."

At first, Peter couldn't be sure he'd heard correctly. "Would ya marry me?" he asked again.

"I said, yes."

"Right now? Tonight?"

Lucy sighed and got to her feet. "Maybe Zack an' Mary still up. Zack, well he the onliest one on the place know how t' marry folk," she explained gently, as though speaking to a petulant child. "If'n ya just cain't wait till tomorrow, we can go see."

Peter grabbed Lucy's hand and pulled her out the door. She got in front of him, just as he was about to bolt up the road. Turning him in the opposite direction, she led the way toward the largest shack in the quarters. Zack had built every bit of it with his own hands, enlarging it as his and Mary's family grew. The place was dark and silent when Lucy and Peter reached it. Lucy tapped lightly at the door; almost immediately, Zack's soft baritone sounded from the other side, "Who there?"

"It's me, Lucy. Sorry t'wake ya up, but I needs ya' help."

Zack opened the door and stood there, filling the frame. He peered at the couple. "What'cha need me t' do?"

"Well," Lucy said, somewhat hesitantly, "Peter an' me, we need t' git married tonight, so he don't have t' go live in the single men's shack. He ain't ready fer that yet, so I'm a keep him wit me."

Zack immediately went back inside and came out carrying a thick, tattered book. He directed Lucy and Peter to stand before him, and then waited. After a few minutes, Mary came outside, wearing a smock over a long loose shift that barely hid her advanced pregnancy. She was carrying a broom.

Zack opened the book to a middle page and, without looking at it, began the marriage ceremony. When he reached the part where an official of the church is supposed to pronounce the couple man and wife, he stopped. Mary placed the broom in front of Peter and Lucy.

"I ain't got no authority t 'nounce ya husband an' wife." Zack said, "But, once't ya jump this here broom, you married, far as anybody concerned."

Peter took Lucy's hand and, together, they jumped. Zack clapped Peter on the back while Mary hugged Lucy. The two women embraced silently for several minutes. Finally they parted and Zack, his arm around Mary's shoulder, shepherded her back inside. Lucy turned to Peter and said, "Let's go home."

And so began a marriage that everyone agreed was one of the best on the farm. For Peter, it was his salvation. When he'd told Lucy he loved her, he'd had no idea whether he was telling the truth; he'd only known, with absolute certainty, that he'd have said anything to get her to let him stay. Later, as they would share their stories of pain and loss, each would heal the other. Peter told Lucy about his first love and the three babies he'd barely gotten to see before being sold off. Lucy told him how she had been coupled at thirteen with a stud Negro whom she'd never met before and would never see again. Later, she and her child from that brief union were separated when the farm where she'd worked and all the slaves were sold off to different buyers.

By the time Lucy became pregnant, Peter had come to realize that love could not begin to describe what he felt for his wife. She was his first thought upon being awakened by the horn. Peter, now watched his daughter, Lucy, who looked so much like her namesake; he could barely believe how the passage of time had done so little to ease his grief and rage. Yet, here she was, his Lucy; she even sounded like her mother.

CHAPTER 23

*T*hey buried Lemuel beside all the others who'd died in service to the land, in a lovely but marshy spot, unsuited for planting anything besides the dead. Quash had led a group of men back to the tree that same afternoon and collected him, thinking that they'd have to hide his body till nightfall.

But Tucker never came back out of his cabin, so they just carried Lemuel out to the workers' graveyard, said a few quick prayers and put him in the ground. By the following morning, it seemed like, everything had returned to normal. Tucker blew the horn at daybreak. Peter assembled the slaves in the clearing near the quarters. And the work commenced as though a death had never occurred.

That month passed and then another. The weather warmed as summer moved into the Hudson valley for her short stay. With the cycle of planting and harvesting in full sway, Tucker had more than enough to concentrate on besides Sally. Yet she sat, always, in the front of his mind.

He understood she was still angry, but now he didn't understand the girl at all. She'd stopped speaking to him, even to answer direct questions. If he came home and asked her what's for supper, she simply pointed to the pot on the hearth and went back to whatever she'd been doing. And she was always doing something – sewing or polishing the tools. If he tried to get her attention or stop her, she'd fix him with a stare so eerie he'd immediately back off and leave her alone.

As for lovemaking, well that had become its own nightmare. Sally would lie beneath him, watching him hump and huff fruitlessly. Even in the darkness, he could feel her eyes, seemingly unblinking, staring into his face. He'd become so unnerved that he'd have to stop, at which point, she'd continue staring until he got off, turned his back on her and went to sleep. Tucker began to dread approaching her. Yet he couldn't stop himself from needing to take her every night.

Sally barely made it out the door before throwing up violently. The mess landed several feet away. Then, she squatted and urinated just as forcefully, pee running round her feet in rivulets. Inside, Tucker had started stirring; she heard his feet hit the floor and the scrape of his shoes as he pulled them from beneath the bed.

The first smears of daylight were just visible through the tree tops, lifting the grey of early dawn. She got herself up and, without wiping anything, picked up the bucket sitting beside the rain barrel and went back to the well.

Drawing water had become so difficult; it seemed the strength had gone right out of her arms. She let the bucket down into cool darkness and leaned briefly against the stone slab she'd propped against a tree. Just before pulling the bucket back up, she bent over the well and tried to peer into its depths.

Wonder how far down it go, she thought. If'n I was t' jump in how long fore I hit water? The idea so appealed to her that she found herself tipping perilously forward. Abruptly, she felt herself jerked backward, whirled around and slapped so hard, she fell to the ground.

"Goddammit!" Tucker shouted, "Goddammit! I gotta watch ya every minute! You was gone jump in the well, wasn't ya!" Breathing hard, he came over to her, lifted her up and held her close. "I ain't meant t' hit'cha, but'cha scared me.

"Sally! Gal, ya gotta git yerself over all a this. Here," he said, gently touching her cheek, which was already becoming purple, "Lemme take care a that swellin."

She twisted out of his embrace. Silently, she took the rope, hauled up the bucket and headed back to the cabin. Once inside, she immediately began preparing Tucker's morning meal. He followed her and sat at the table silently waiting until she served him the cornmeal mush.

Standing at the table, watching him eat, Sally asked herself why she hadn't done what Tucker so obviously feared she would. The desire stayed so strong in her, yet she just couldn't bring herself to violently end two lives.

The pregnancy must've begun sometime during last winter, Sally wasn't sure. But this time, she was sick every morning and had been, seemingly for months. Moreover, she wasn't growing the way she normally did, so she really couldn't tell how far along she was. One thing she was sure of, though, was that there was no way she was telling Master Tucker about any baby!

That night in the darkness, Sally pushed Tucker's arm off her waist and got up. She stood beside the bed for a long time listening to his breathing. For a while after Lemuel's death, he'd slept badly, tossing about and nearly knocking her out of bed more than once. But now he seemed to have settled back into his old pattern; he wouldn't move until daybreak.

She pulled on her blouse and skirt, tied on her head wrap and slipped out. The once so familiar route through the forest had grown new tangled underbrush that caught the hem of her skirt and nearly tripped her up several times. When, she finally stumbled out of the woods, she was right behind the single men's shack. Here, her feet slowed of their own accord and she gazed at it. The building seemed more ramshackle than ever; most of the boards on the back wall were now completely missing. Once, as they lay outside together, hidden by trees and bushes, Sally had asked Lemuel whether any of the men ever tried to escape through those openings into the woods. "Oh, Sally," he'd laughed in a whisper, "these niggers all too scared t' run!"

She roused herself and headed toward Mary's cabin. Pushing the door open, she tried to see into the darkness.

"Who's there?" Mary whispered, getting up stiffly from her pallet and padding barefoot to the door.

"It's me. Sally" she answered, surprised at the sound of her own voice, how hoarse and cracked it was – like an old woman's. She only now realized that she hadn't spoken in months.

Mary came close. "Sally?" She peered into the girl's face. "What'cha doin here?"

"Come t' see Polly – an the rest a m' chil'ren."

Mary went back into the mass of sleeping children, lifted one and carried her over to Sally, who'd sunk to the floor and now sat with her legs spread apart like a child's. Polly didn't arouse, even when Sally pulled her onto her lap, rocked her and kissed the little girl's opened mouth. Meanwhile, Mary went for a candle. Something about Sally clearly wasn't right.

In the flickering light, Mary was shocked at the girl's appearance. Sally was obviously pregnant, but much too thin. The baby sat in a small ball, tight and low in her belly. Her breasts were nearly flat. And Mary could see the girl's bones.

"Sally! What happened? Masta Tucker stop feedin ya?" Mary kept her voice low, but couldn't hide her alarm.

Sally smiled slowly, her lips pulling at the edges until teeth showed. "Well, he been tryin t' tempt me t' eat more. Say I'm gittin too skinny. He tryin' all kinda ways. Brought me a whole side a hog, what he done. I butchered the whole thing an' fed it t' him. Ain't et none! Not one bit!" She cackled softly. "Here, take Polly on back an' bring me the other ones."

Mary lifted the child and placed her back between her sleeping mates. Then Mary moved to another pallet and roused the oldest child. Placing her finger to her lips, she whispered something to the girl, who promptly pulled two more children from their sleeping places. Li'l Mary, as Sally's first born was now known, herded Sarah and Zack toward the front of the cabin. Mary followed with Simon and Tom. They stood in a row before their mother, all more asleep than awake, except Li'l Mary. Sally surveyed her brood, still smiling somewhat crookedly.

"C'mere. Lemme hug alla ya."

Li'l Mary looked at Mary, who gestured them forward. The girl somewhat tentatively pulled her siblings along and they all crowded onto Sally's lap. She wrapped her arms around them and then kissed each one.

"Alla ya be good chil'ren. Mind Aint Mary now." Sally let her children go.

Li'l Mary lingered behind even after Mary had settled the others. She stood just behind Mary staring avidly at this woman who Aint Mary had told her was her "Ma'am." Li'l Mary didn't remember anything about her. But Aint Mary had said she was "real pretty." This woman didn't look pretty at all! Finally, unable to contain herself, the child spoke up.

"Aint Mary say you our ma'am. How come we don't never see you?"

Mary answered quickly, "Now I explained all a that t' ya!"

"You belongs t' the man what own this farm," Sally said softly. "The ovaseer made me give alla ya up when you was still babes, 'cause he say I couldn't keep ya. An' he don't let me go near ya or the other workers a tall."

Mary interrupted, "Now, Li'l Mary, that's enough. You just go on back t' bed. Yer ma'am come t' see ya an' that's more'n a lot a chil'ren git what ain't wit they folks!"

Li'l Mary dropped her head. Sullenly, she headed back to the pallet she shared with her sister and brothers. She had been wishing for so long to have a chance to see her mother, expecting somehow to recognize and love her immediately. She felt bitterly disappointed. This woman was nothing more than a stranger.

Once the children were down, Mary came back to where Sally still sat, now seemingly spent. She drew up a low stool and set the candlestick on the floor beside her.

"Chile, how far along are ya?"

"Don't rightly know this time. It just sorta happened. Maybe winter, early winter."

"Well that mean y' aughta be a lot bigger'n ya are."

Sally didn't answer, just closed her eyes.

"Think I'm a ask Masta Tucker can I look in on ya from time t' time. Ya don't look good, Sally. This not eatin', it ain't gone do you nor the babe no good!"

"Masta Tucker don't know I'm expectin."

Mary sat up straight, aghast. "How that possible? I seen it right off! How he miss it?"

Sally didn't try to explain. She had made Tucker afraid to even look directly at her. It hadn't been deliberate; she hadn't planned her actions. Something, some inner power seemed to be compelling her – the same force that kept her silent and unwilling to eat. She got slowly to her feet.

"I got t' git back."

"I'm a speak t' Masta Tucker first chance I git. If'n he don't know yet, he will. Ya need t'be taken care of."

"It don't matter if'n ya tell Masta Tucker now or not. It's too late fer him t' do anything about it anyways." Sally stepped across the open door sill and melted into the night.

CHAPTER 24

*L*ittle Polly was growing up like a weed. Untended by anyone in particular – Mary had so many other children to
look after – she'd always go her own way. As far as everyone was
concerned, her mother and a twin had died in childbirth. Now
nearly two, she ran about on tiny sturdy legs after any of the
several flocks of children who spent their days playing in Mary's
front yard.

Polly, like her actual sisters and brothers, had Sally's wide eyed
gaze and perfect oval face. It would not have taken close scrutiny
to spot the resemblance between them. But, because she was the
color of mahogany with a close cap of wooly hair while the others
were all caramel hued with hair that was black and curly or wavy,
no one ever did. And Mary had made sure to keep all the children
ignorant about the relationship.

Li'l Mary, as unofficial child-minder and Mary's special help-
er, usually made sure that the little ones stayed out of trouble.
She especially liked taking care of Polly. The little girl minded so
much better than her brothers and sister had. Gradually the older
child and the younger one developed a bond that even the threat
of the fields couldn't break. For Li'l Mary was surely destined for
the fields, if not this year than the next, when she'd be eight. She
was already a full head taller than any of the other children still
under Mary's care.

To get the girl ready, Mary had gradually added to Li'l Mary's list of chores. She was still responsible for gathering eggs, but now it was from all the hen houses. In addition, after the sheep had been sheared, she had to gather the washed wool and get the smaller children to help her with the carding – combing the fibrous wool into separate strands that would then be spun into yarn for weaving. Li'l Mary made up games, pitting the boys against the girls to see who could card wool the fastest or gather the most eggs without breaking any. There'd be much fussing amongst the girls, sitting together with their hair all festooned in wooly wisps, while the boys would push each other and fight over the cards. Invariably, much of the wool would get dirty again. And, as they ran in and out of the hen houses carrying egg baskets, all of the children managed to drop almost as many eggs as they gathered.

Even though still a toddler, Polly joined in avidly. But instead of simply playing at the chores, she actually tried to do them right. She'd stand close next to Li'l Mary, watching until she could almost approximate the task, then she'd try with all her might to copy the older girl's movements. Eventually Li'l Mary took to keeping Polly beside her all day long.

"Look like some a yer charges gittin big enough fer the fields."

Mary had been standing in her yard watching the children play during the last hour before their parents came to claim them for the night. The voice behind her came so suddenly that she actually jumped.

"Peter! Didn't hear ya come up."

"Ain't meant t' scare ya. Just noticin how them chil'ren the ovaseer whelped is gittin big now. Bout time fer some of um t' git t' workin." Peter came and stood beside Mary as he spoke.

Mary turned to face him. For several moments she hesitated, weighing the wisdom of broaching the one topic that neither of them wanted to raise. At last she lifted her chin, steadied herself and spoke up. "Peter, I know you knowed 'bout Sally an' Lemuel. Was it you told Masta Tucker?"

Peter's lips tightened into a thin, pursed line. His eyes narrowed almost menacingly. "How you come t' ask me that? You think I'd do such a thing? Long as you been knowin' me – an' m' Lucy, what that man done t' us both! Ya' think fer one minute I'd tell that man a goddamn thing?"

Mary reached out both hands, gripping Peter's elbows. "Naw, Peter, I ain't forgot nothing! It just, ya made Lemuel an' Sally stop seeing one 'nother. An' now, well, I ain't sure that were such a good idea. Lemuel dead an' I'm afeared Sally grieving too hard. Y' know I'm the onliest one been able t' see her an' she lookin real bad now. She expectin' again, too."

"Well, as to me stoppin' them from seein' one 'nother, I guess that's what she told ya' I done. An' I ain't gone lie 'bout it. Maybe I was wrong, but cain't nothin be changed now." Peter took a step closer; his voice dropped to a whisper. "There is one thing, though – Sally's *other* babe. Ya' gotta keep that one hid real good,' specially if'n it be a gal. A gal of Sally's sure t' favor her ma. Masta Tucker see her, t' won't be good fer nobody!" He turned and headed off toward his own shack.

After the last of her charges had been picked up, Mary gathered her own brood – Sally's six, plus two babies and three more small children who stayed with her – and settled them around her table for supper. There wasn't enough room at the actual table or space on the one bench for everyone, but the larger children had been trained to hold the smallest ones on their laps and help with the feeding. Li'l Mary supervised, moving around among the children, with Polly clinging to the hem of her skirt with one small hand.

Before serving the meal, Mary stood at the head of the table and commanded that everyone hold hands as she gave the blessing. These prayers were always improvised, a combination of thanks for the food, moral lessons and specific warnings against any bad behavior Li'l Mary had reported to her that day – with the name of the perpetrator always pointedly inserted. On this evening, however, Mary wandered from her usual text.

"Dear Lord an' Savior, Jesus Christ, we thank ya' fer the food we 'bout t' receive," she began in the usual way. Then, "Dear Lord, send yer protection round this house an' all a us what dwell herein. Keep what need t' be hidden hid. An' keep all pryin' eyes away." Her voice became louder, more urgent. "Stop the ears of the wicked an' still they lyin' tongues! Keep the evil away from these poor chil'ren, Oh Lord, our strength an' our Redeemer!"

Mary finished and glanced round the table. Eleven wide, clearly frightened sets of eyes were fixed on her. She quickly gathered herself and began ladling out greens and corn meal mush. Within minutes all the children were eating their first and only meal of the day, their fears forgotten. As they ate, Mary silently continued her prayer, "An' Lord, please help me find some kinda way t' help that poor chile, Sally!"

The following evening, she left Li'l Mary in charge of bedding everyone down after supper and took the short path down the row to Peter's shack. Lucy answered her knock and came to the door.

"Why, Miz Mary! Weren't expectin t' see you this time a night." The young woman's puzzled smile ushered Mary inside.

"Well, y' know this the onliest time anybody can git together. An I needs t' speak wit' cha pa."

"He takin his evenin walk. He be back directly. Ya wanna wait fer him?" Lucy cleared a pile of mending off the bench to make space for Mary to sit.

"Thankee Chile." Mary took the seat offered, just as the door opened and Peter entered.

His eyes registered momentary surprise. But almost as quickly, he greeted her as though he'd been anticipating the visit. He asked his daughter to step outside for a few minutes. Lucy, accustomed to her father's sometimes inexplicable moods, quickly picked up the water bucket and left.

Mary took a deep breath to steady her nerves a bit. "Peter," she began carefully, "Bout what'cha was sayin' before, what'cha mean by Sally's other chile? Whoever say she got some chile ain't been counted fer?"

"Listen, Mary," Peter came and sat next to her on the bench. "Ya ain't gotta lie t' me 'bout Sally an' Lemuel's chile. I knowed 'bout it from the first. An' they both knowed I did." He stopped abruptly, then continued after a moment, "None a that don't matter no more now. What do matter is keepin' Masta Tucker from seeing the chile fer as long as we can. What I wanna do is t'git that oldest gal a'his out in the fields soon as possible. He ain't gone wanna see her too much, I betcha. Just remind him what he don't own. He won't wanna be watchin the rest a'the slaves so close then neither; he'll let me do that."

A silence fell between them. Mary smoothed the course fabric of her skirt, picking absently at knotted threads in the weave. At last, she stood up. "Li'l Mary really should wait fer the next plantin' season. She tall, but not real strong. Her brother Zack could go now, maybe. He a lot shorter, but he real sturdy. They all too young though, tell the truth."

"Yeah, but the longer we wait, the more time niggers got t' talk amongst theyselves. An' Masta Tucker been actin' real queer. He following people 'round all the time tryin' t' hear what they sayin'. Seem like, since he found out 'bout Lemuel, he think everybody keepin' secrets." Peter's voice had taken on the same hard edge Mary had noticed when he'd spoken about the overseer the day before.

"Well, do what'cha think best," she said at last and rose to take her leave.

"So it's settled then." Peter said, walking her to the door, "Tomorrow, want 'cha t' send out Li'l Mary when the horn sound. Don'tcha worry 'bout her. I'll see t' it she don't git worked too hard."

CHAPTER 25

The pain came on sudden and hard. Sally had been outside gathering wood when she doubled up and her legs gave way. Getting clumsily to her knees, she braced herself and tried to stand, only to have another agonizing wave knock her flat again. This time she stayed down until that pain passed. Then she crawled slowly back to the cabin door, stopping to breathe through the next contraction. She hadn't made any provisions for the baby to be coming this quick.

Tucker was at the door, ready to leave for the day. He ran out, hurriedly gathered her up and rushed her inside. Depositing her on the bed, he demanded to know why she'd been on the ground.

"Ya' fell? You sick or what?"

Sally turned away. For a long moment, Tucker stood over the bed, waiting. Just as he was about to give up – she never answered him anyway – she suddenly spoke.

"Ya need t' git Miz Mary."

"Why?"

"I'm 'bout t' have a babe."

The overseer stood there thunderstruck. Then he stammered something about "Stay where yer at! I'll be right back!" and ran out, the door slamming behind him. His leaving seemed to sweep out the darkness that had collected around her for so long.

Sally sat up and stretched out her bony arms, turning them

this way and that, studying the now visible veins. She brought both palms to her cheeks and gently felt her face. Since becoming Tucker's woman, she hadn't once thought about what she looked like. She waited through another contraction, then got off the bed and walked unsteadily across the room.

Hanging behind the door was a small looking glass that Tucker used on the rare occasions when he shaved himself. She would never even glance at it. Today, however, she made her way to the spot where it hung at eye level for the overseer but just above her head.

She dragged Tucker's chair to the wall and crawled up onto the seat. She could only manage to get to her knees but it was just enough for her to see her face.

Sally started to laugh. The reflection was absolutely unrecognizable! This was what Tucker had been lusting after all these years? Sunken cheeks, ashy black skin! Eyes too big for her face! Hair un-plaited and standing every which way! Her laughter became hysterical and she collapsed onto the chair, then slipped off the seat and fell to the floor where she lay as waves of contractions washed over her.

Sally just about to give birth! Tucker had had no idea she was even pregnant. Now, he didn't stop running till he'd reached Mary's shack. Stopping only long enough to catch his breath, he pushed he door open. The children were just beginning to stir and the youngest were still asleep. Mary was pulling a shirt over the head of one small boy whose mother had just left.

"Mary!" Tucker shouted. "Yer gone have t' leave these li'l niggers alone fer a spell an come wit me! Sally say she bout t' drop my chile an I don't wanna lose this one! So come on right now!"

With a troubled backward glance at her sleeping charges, Mary hurried out after him. She called to the lone boy standing close to the road, "Zack! Yer in charge till I git back! Don't let none'a them chil'ren git near the fire! Ya hear me?"

"Yes ma'am, Aint Mary," the child answered morosely as he turned and headed back toward the shack.

Mary couldn't keep up with the overseer – the man was covering so much distance with each stride. Halfway up the road, he suddenly turned back and shouted for her to catch up. Then he resumed his headlong pace, reaching his cabin door well ahead of her.

Tucker stopped, pushed open the door and then just stood there. When Mary finally got to the open door, she rushed in past him. Sally was lying in a pool of blood on the floor. Mary lifted the girl's skirts and there, between Sally's open legs, was a miniature infant, still attached to its umbilical cord. The tiny, pale thing, no bigger than a man's hand, wasn't moving. Mary went for a knife to cut the cord.

Getting down stiffly, she lifted the baby gingerly and turned it face down, feeling for signs of breath. Then she held it up by its heels and stroked its back with one finger. Finally, she severed the cord and stood up slowly. Holding the infant in both palms, she presented it to Tucker.

"Sorry, Masta," she said, simply.

Tucker took a step back and then another. He kept backing up till he was outside the door and on the road. Mary watched him stumble, catch himself, half turn and run off. Then she retuned to the tasks at hand. She bathed the tiny body, wrapped it in a towel and laid it on the table. Next she tried to rouse Sally. The young woman must have fainted during the birth, but she should have come awake by now.

Sally didn't respond when Mary first tried patting her face. Finally, Mary slapped her and Sally's eyelids fluttered. She tried to sit up but quickly fell back. Mary caught her by the shoulders and, struggling against the girl's almost dead weight, dragged her over to the bed. Mary was finally able to get Sally up on her feet. As soon as she did, Sally fell face down across the bed. Mary had to turn her over and swing her around so that she was lying properly at last.

"Chile," the older woman gasped, breathing heavily from the exertion, "What'cha done t' yerself? An' this babe? Told you ya' needed t' take better care'a yerself. Now, ya' done lost this last one."

Sally opened her eyes and smiled. "I starved it, what I done," she whispered. "Told ya' I weren't havin no more babies fer Masta Tucker."

"Oh, Chile! Now why ya' gone an' done that? Don'tcha know ya' cain't starve no babe what's inside a' ya' witout starvin' yerself?"

"Yeah, I know. That's what I done." Sally closed her eyes again.

Mary decided there was nothing she could do other than to clean Sally up and make her as comfortable as possible. She undid Sally's bloody skirt and slipped it off, followed by her soiled petticoat and shift. She brought the basin over to the bed and washed off as much of the afterbirth as she could. As she did so, Mary tried not to flinch at the visible hip bones and skeletal thighs.

How could Master Tucker not have seen Sally getting this thin right before his very eyes? The ovaseer must be gittin' crazy like everybody sayin' he is, Mary decided as she watched Sally lying there so very quiet. The girl neither moved nor opened her eyes again. Finally Mary got up to leave.

"Well, he seen this one's dead, so I might as well take it wit me," she said aloud, as she gathered up the dirty clothing. Then she carefully centered the wrapped-up baby on the pile of clothes, bundled everything together and slipped out, closing the door softly behind her.

Tucker spent over an hour walking the road between the quarters and the nearest fields. This couldn't be happening again! The overseer wanted to go back to his cabin and see about Sally but he just couldn't stop his feet from moving first in one direction on the road, and then in reverse.

Everything was falling apart! Sally wouldn't have anything to do with him, couldn't give him children. And now, thanks to killing Lemuel, he was penniless. As it turns out, Mr. Firth had made a full deduction of the cost of the dead slave from Tucker's annual salary for the next ten years!

Tucker was never going be free of the debt nor of this job. He would never be able to even dream of becoming a tenant farmer with his own slave woman and children who could work alongside him. His heart felt like it was in a vice and he could hardly breathe.

The sun was already high and the day's work had begun, thanks to Peter's assembling everyone and setting up the various gangs. Tucker knew he needed to at least make an appearance in one of the fields but, try as he might, he just couldn't calm himself. He was still pacing wildly when he finally heard the voice shouting his name.

The teamsters' wagon had pulled up on the main road and one of the men had come out to find him. This team of drivers was new to the circuit of farms and, having never visited this one, was therefore unknown to Tucker. He had, in fact completely forgotten about the scheduled visit.

"Martin Tucker!" the bandy-legged fellow heading toward him shouted. "Where was ya'? We been all over this place lookin' fer a white man! Niggers told us they ain't seen ya' all morning! We gotta git yer provision off'a our wagon! Ain't cha got produce t' git out? Where's yer men at?"

Tucker was jerked out of his fog as though someone had dashed cold water all over him. He stammered "I-I-weren't expectin' ya' till next week."

"That ain't what we was told. Mr. Firth, he told us t' keep t' the regular schedule, just like the old drivers. An' that's just what we done. First'a the month. That's when they always come. Today's the first'a the month!"

The driver kept up a steady stream of criticisms and observations as he followed the overseer down the road toward the nearest field. Tucker struggled to corral his thoughts around the necessary jobs at hand. Keeping the delivery schedule was his responsibility alone; Peter only supervised the workers.

Usually, he'd remind Peter to have workers assembled at the barns for unloading provisions and loading produce. Today, he'd have to find Peter first; yet he had no idea where the man was.

He finally found Peter working alongside a gang gathering sheaves of wheat in the farthest field from the road. The wheat stood taller than the workers' heads and at first Tucker wasn't sure whether Peter was in this group.

"You! Niggers!"

Everyone stopped work and turned in Tucker's direction. Peter stepped away from the group and headed toward the overseer.

"Need ya' t' git a gang together t' take care'a the supply wagon."

Peter pointed wordlessly to the ten men nearest him. They silently lined up and followed the overseer and the driver, who was still carrying on under his breath about hired hands who make everybody else late because they can't keep to schedules.

Back at the barns, the teamsters walked around, stretching their legs while the workers unloaded the wagon, carried the provisions inside and stored everything. Then, it was out to the sheds where the grain had been bundled, ready to be loaded into the now nearly empty wagon. There were half a dozen head of fattened beef cattle ready for market, along with several crates of live chickens and ducks. These crates the workers also loaded; the cattle would be driven along behind the wagon.

Tucker supervised the start of the work, indicating where things should be placed; then he went into a nearby shack and reappeared with a jug.

"Thought'cha might be needin' a nip, just t' pass the time whilst the wagon's bein' loaded up," Tucker said as he handed the jug to Bandy Legs. "Might make up a bit fer the time ya' lost lookin' fer me."

He watched the man take a long draw and then pass the jug to his two companions. They passed the jug between them for four more rounds before handing it back to the overseer. This batch of corn mash was freshly made – just strained and not distilled – and easily consumed without getting particularly drunk.

Tucker had often wished he could build a proper still for making real spirits, but, whenever he'd approached Mr. Firth with the idea, the accountant had always become quite short, stiffly reminding him that "It isn't your place to make such suggestions. You know nothing whatsoever about Mr. Van Driessen's business interests!"

The teamsters had drained the jug before handing it back to Tucker. By this time the wagon was loaded up and the cattle were ready for the drive. Two of the men mounted the wagon, while the third, long switch in hand, prepared to walk behind the animals. Each of the teamsters would take his turn herding the cattle over the twenty or so miles back to Albany.

Once they'd gone, Tucker went back into the shed and emerged with another jug. He motioned to the workers who were now standing around waiting for their next orders.

"All'a ya', just go on back t' whatever ya' was doin' before."

Effectively dismissed, the ten men meandered off in different directions. Only one dared look back over his shoulder. He would later report to the other workers that he'd seen, with his own eyes, Tucker raise the jug to his lips and apparently drain the thing. And then the overseer had sat himself down beside the shed and dropped off to sleep.

CHAPTER 26

a blaze of sunlight burned, even through closed eyelids, so Sally kept them shut tight. She felt hot and cold at the same time, but also weightless – as though she were about to float away. She lifted both arms without effort, letting them rise above her horizontal body. The bed was still under her, but there seemed to be a cushion of air between her and the hard mattress. Clearly, something was happening to her, something wonderful....

Suddenly, she was no longer inside Tucker's cabin; she was back on the old farm. The afternoon sun was so hot and the workers needed water almost constantly. She was supposed to be fetching another bucket, but instead, she'd coaxed Lemuel to slip way with her for a quick game of hide-and-seek.

"*Saalleee.*" The voice came gentle, teasing. "*I'm'a find ya', Sally. Ya know ya' cain't hide from me.*" Lemuel's face appeared suddenly, just above hers.

"Oh, Lemuel, how come ya' always know where I'm hidin'?"

He had lifted the cover to the root cellar and now was standing right over her. She raised a small hand. "Well! Ya' kin just help me up then!"

A corona of sunlight blazed all around him. Sally tried to focus on his face as she begged this time, "Help me up, Lemuel."

"*Sally. I'm'a take yer hand. An', this time, I ain't never lettin' go again. You want me t' do that? Are ya' sure ya' ready?*"

She could see him clearly now. He wasn't the skinny-legged eight year-old who'd always come find her when he was supposed to be in the fields. He was grown. His face, square-jawed and wide-eyed seemed aglow. He was grinning with that gap-toothed grin of his.

"I'm ready," she answered and took his outstretched hand.

Purple evening shadows had long ago descended over the quarters. Workers had been back in their shacks since before sundown. After all, Tucker never reappeared and Peter had simply let everyone go home. In Mary's shack, all the other children had been picked up and only her charges were left. She fed them and sent them all to bed. Then, she pulled on a tattered shawl and slipped out.

Misgivings dogged her every step as she made her way toward Tucker's cabin. She'd only been there after dark during Sally's illness, and that had been at the overseer's insistence. Now she was coming unannounced. At the door, she stopped and placed one hand against the wooden planks. Something was preventing her opening that door – something palpable and cold.

She backed away, turned and fled in the direction she'd come from. Once safely inside her own shack, Mary chided herself. Just bein' silly, what I'm doin! Tomorrow, first thing I'm goin' back up there. An' this time, I'm goin' in!

Li'l Mary had awakened when she'd heard Mary leave. Polly now slept right next to Li'l Mary and she'd awakened too.

"Where Aint Mary goin'?" the little girl asked, rubbing sleep out of her eyes.

"Shhh!" Li'l Mary whispered, a finger to her lips, "She just goin' outside. Lay back down."

Polly did so and was almost immediately sleeping soundly again. Li'l Mary, however, couldn't manage to fall back to sleep, no matter how hard she tried. For the longest, she tried to figure out what it was – the strange unsettled feeling in her stomach. Finally, she decided she needed to urinate. Suddenly, the urge became overwhelming.

Pushing the layers of covers aside, she crawled out from between Polly and Zack and just made it outside. She was still squatting beside the shack when, looking up, she saw Mary come down the road, quietly open the door and let herself inside. Li'l Mary hurriedly finished up and was about to rush in behind the old woman, but a peculiar feeling caused her to pause.

Something's wrong, she thought, Aint Mary wasn't just outside doin her business; she went somewhere. But, there was nowhere to go this time of night. Li'l Mary couldn't think of a time when Aint Mary had ever gone out so late. The girl waited at the door until she could no longer hear Mary's movements; then she slipped in and crawled back into her space. Now that she was working the fields, Li'l Mary understood, for the first time really, how long the day could be and how tired she was; she quickly fell asleep. Dawn would come all too soon.

Darkness had fallen long ago when Tucker finally awakened. He'd managed to consume several jugs of the corn mash and was at last drunk. He knew he should get back to the cabin, but Sally was there. The thought of her just made him wish for more whisky, so he got up and stumbled back into the shed. Once he'd found the remaining jugs, he settled himself into a corner for the rest of the night.

Just before daybreak, the cocks started their crowing, a sign for Peter to get up and blow the horn. He came outside barefoot, took up the battered bugle and sounded a long blast. Immediately there was stirring in each of the shacks. Peter went back in, put on thick stockings and shoes and came back out.

Sleepy men, women and children had assembled in the open area just beyond the quarters. He called out names and field assignments. There was corn ready for harvest, a perfect job for the children. The several younger ones, along with Li'l Mary, were given the task of pulling the lowest ears, which they would drop into small sacks worn like bandoliers across their bodies. Once the gangs had been formed, everyone marched off.

About an hour later, Tucker appeared in one of the fields, red-eyed and disheveled. He'd gotten one of the horses and ridden out to find the workers. Everyone looked up at his approach and then quickly went back to work. He continued on to the next field, and the one adjacent to that. Finally, he found Peter in a rye field supervising the harvest. Tucker nodded briefly and Peter immediately took up his scythe and began cutting sheaves alongside another man.

At about the same time, Mary, her daytime charges temporarily under Zack's less-than-able care, had finally gotten back to the overseer's cabin. She knocked on the door, softly at first, then more loudly. When there was still no response, she pushed it open.

The air inside was still and stale-smelling. The room was exactly as she had left it, nothing moved, no evidence that Tucker had come back to check on Sally at all.

Sally was still on the bed in exactly the position she'd been in when Mary had left her the day before. And that was what was so very troubling. The girl should have moved – or at least shifted position.

Suddenly frightened, Mary approached the bed. Sally lay on her back, neatly covered, arms at her sides, eyes closed, just as Mary had left her the day before. Little had the woman known when she'd bathed and dressed Sally that she would now find her already laid out for burial.

When Mary touched the girl's cheek, it was cold. Mary gently took the top edge of the blanket and drew it over Sally's face. Then she left the cabin to go find the overseer.

Tucker took the news of Sally's death badly. First, in disbelief, he spurred his horse into a gallop and raced back to his cabin. Dismounting, he crashed through the door, almost taking the thing off its hinges.

When he saw his girl's covered body, he sank to his knees, howling so loudly and for so long that some of the women spinning in a shed a short distance away from the cabin came to investigate.

They all went running back to their companions with the news. In short order, everyone on the farm knew that the overseer's woman was dead.

CHAPTER 27

Eighteen years after Sally's death, there had been changes in the Van Driessen's family holdings. The ownership had changed hands, and the old reverend's grandson inherited the several properties from his father. This grandson then sold off two of the smaller farms to his equally wealthy neighbor and allowed a tenant farmer to work the third small farm. This left Petrus Van Driessen III with two remaining properties, the Albany estate where he resided, and the large farm where Tucker remained on as overseer.

The young Van Driessen, unlike his predecessors, took a personal interest in his properties. Soon after taking ownership, he made it his business to visit the farm in the company of his father's accountant, the now-elderly Jason Firth.

The two men arrived about mid-morning in Van Driessen's coach, driven by his personal servant, a rather portly middle-aged Negro who doubled as the footman. The two horses pulled up in front of the overseer's cabin and the servant got down first, then went round and opened the coach door so both men could alight.

By the time they'd arrived, the day's work was well underway and, therefore no one was about to direct the young owner and his small entourage. Mr. Firth moved stiffly – he now had rheumatism and the ride had been most uncomfortable. The coach horses had managed to take them over every rock and boulder between here and Albany. But Van Driessen was only 23; he'd barely felt the many bumps and was eager to get a feel for this place.

"I say, Firth!" he called out cheerily, "What say we go and find this overseer. What's his name?"

"Martin Tucker," the accountant replied, somewhat peevishly. "Had you allowed me to send word of our visit beforehand, I daresay he'd have been on hand to greet us properly!"

"Nonsense!" came the breezy reply. "I didn't want the man to put on a show for my benefit. I want to see things as they are on a regular day, with no special preparations made!"

Mr. Firth sniffed in annoyance as the young Van Driessen set off on foot. "If you don't mind, I'll just wait here in the carriage. You! Caesar! Help me up into this damned thing!"

The slave roused himself and quickly took the accountant's arm, allowing the man to lean heavily on him as he mounted the single steep step. Mr. Firth finally settled himself inside on the coach seat, took off his wig and attempted to shake some of the road dust out of it. It was an old-fashioned, full-powdered affair that reached to his shoulders. He never wore his wig when he knew he had to visit the farms; the trip was much too dusty! But the young Mr. Van Driessen had pulled a surprise on him with this trip.

After about half an hour of wandering, Van Driessen finally located Tucker, on horseback heading in his direction.

"I say! Might you be the overseer?"

"I am. An' who might ya' be?" Tucker said as he reared his horse to a stop a short distance away. "I weren't expectin' no white-er-gentleman visitor."

Van Driessen drew himself up to his full height. Without removing his obviously expensive three-corner hat, he replied coolly, "I am Mr. Petrus Van Driessen III Esq. your employer. No doubt Mr. Firth has mentioned the family's name in his dealings with you. As I have recently inherited, I intend to make a tour of the facilities. You are to conduct myself and Mr. Firth forthwith."

Tucker immediately pulled off his own straw hat, at the same time running his free hand through now salt-and-pepper, shoulder-length hair. Dismounting, he made a quick, awkward bow. "Beggin' yer pardon, Sir. If I'd a knowed ya' was comin', I'd been at the gate t' meet 'cha. Where the other mens at, Sir?

"My coach and footman are on the road in front of your cabin. Mr. Firth also remained behind. If you would help me mount up, I intend to ride back with you."

The two men remained where they were for another full second. Then Tucker walked his horse over to Van Driessen. The young man was nearly a head shorter than the overseer, but a bit on the stout side. Tucker knelt in the dirt and made a cradle of both hands for Van Driessen to use as a step up into the stirrups.

In spite of his weight, the young man mounted easily, took up the reins and offered a hand up to Tucker. Together, they rode back to the cabin. Once there, Van Driessen dismounted easily and, without waiting for Caesar to get down from his seat and come round to help his master, got back into the coach.

Tucker, on horseback, directed the coach and passengers over the length and breadth of the farm. They visited the dairy and granary, the wellhouse and tannery, the grist mill and bakehouse – to observe the baking of the hard tack that was a major product of the farm. They even stopped at the chicken coops so Van Driessen could count the roosters and laying hens. Finally, they wound up at the fields, where Van Driessen once again alighted from the coach and walked among the rows of wheat, corn, oats and rye.

The young owner's gaze was interrupted by the presence of several unusually light-skinned slaves swinging scythes in the wheat field. He called out to no one in particular, "Who are those workers? They're nearly white!"

Mr. Firth answered, "The overseer whelped them. I believe there are six of them in total."

Van Driessen turned around slowly and gave Tucker a cool appraising stare. After several rather uncomfortable seconds, during which the overseer could feel himself becoming hot and angry, Tucker finally spoke.

"I-I- They was from when I had taken in one a' the womens, sir. They belongs t' you."

"Well they appear to be quite grown up now. Why didn't you have more? Oh wait!" Van Driessen suddenly whirled and faced the accountant. "Mr. Firth, didn't you say that this man had purchased his woman some years ago?" Now the young man swung round to face the overseer yet again. "I should think you've managed to whelp some servants of your own by now."

Tucker couldn't safely respond. He dropped to one knee and pretended to examine a clump of dirt. With head bowed, he struggled to regain enough composure not to grab this insufferable little man by the throat and choke him until his eyes bulged out!

Finally, it was Mr. Firth who spoke, "Mr. Van Driessen, I do believe the unfortunate girl died in childbirth some years ago. Sadly, Mr. Tucker, here, had not quite finished paying for her when she passed. Also, Mr. Tucker did cause the death of one of your workers and is paying for that one also."

Van Driessen appeared to have lost interest in Mr. Firth's lengthy explanation. Shading his eyes with one gloved hand, he peered out across the field, then walked a few feet, apparently searching for something.

"How many did you say there were?" he suddenly enquired, obviously speaking to the accountant, although never addressing the man directly.

"I believe there are six – or perhaps five."

"Well," Van Driessen continued, "As you know, I'm to marry within the fortnight. I shall certainly need additional servants for my wife, and at the new house. Those light-skinned ones could fit the bill quite nicely, provided they're quick-witted enough."

The young man suddenly turned toward Tucker. "Have the ones I've indicated brought up to your cabin immediately. We'll have a look at them. If they pass muster, we can use one of the wagons to bring them along to town." Fully satisfied with his inspection of the farm and with himself for solving the servant problem so neatly, Van Driessen returned to his coach. He called out to his man, "Caesar! When we get back to this man's cabin, you are to go with him to select a suitable sized wagon, which you will drive back to Albany. Mr. Firth and I will drive the coach."

Tucker had gotten to his feet by this time. He mounted his horse silently and led the way back to his cabin. There, without dismounting, he galloped off to find Peter. Peter could notify the slaves about their impending change of fortune.

Actually, Tucker had never even spoken directly to any of his children, since he'd never considered them his. In this, he was quite correct, as Van Driessen had made abundantly clear this morning. Sally's five children were now going to become house servants, living in a city where people wore nice clothing and ate foods he'd never even heard of. In truth, Tucker had no real idea about the life his children were about to embark upon. He just knew it would be infinitely better than his own.

He found Peter in one of the barns attached to the dairy. Here women milked the cows, churned butter and made cheese. Tucker found the man examining a cow's swollen udder.

"Been lookin' all over fer ya." The overseer began, "Need fer ya' t 'round up the five light-skinned niggers an bring them up t' my cabin. Drop what'cha doin an tend t' this right now."

Peter wordlessly walked out of the barn, leaving Tucker standing there. The overseer rubbed the back of his neck in irritation. Seemed like everybody was bent on disrespecting him today. But, he was more or less used to Peter's silent contempt. The man knew he drank too much and was too frequently late getting to the fields. Yet Peter kept everyone working and the farm producing. If he no longer bothered to acknowledge Tucker's presence, at least he still followed direct orders.

Li'l Mary was wielding her scythe one row over from her brother Zack. Now in her twenties, she was one of the best female workers on the place, able to cut nearly her weight in wheat or rye on any day. At first, she didn't hear when Peter shouted her name. It was only after the third time that she looked up.

"Masta Tucker want'cha t' come wit' me." Peter said, approaching through the waving wheat stalks, "Where yer brothers at? An' yer sister?"

"Zack right over there," Li'l Mary straightened up and pointed to the next row, "Don't know where Simon an' Tom at, but Sarah in the bakehouse today."

Peter shouted, "Zack!" and a tall young man straighten up, his head just clearing the tops of the stalks. He immediately pushed his way through and came to stand beside his sister. The two were almost identical, both in coloring and attractiveness. Peter repeated his instructions that they follow him as he led the way out of the fields. At the bakehouse, they collected Sarah, a slightly shorter version of her brother and sister.

"Go on up the road till ya' git t' Masta Tucker place. Wait over there till I git back," Peter said. Then he left the siblings and went to find the remaining two brothers.

It took a complete circuit of all the fields to finally locate Tom and Simon. Tom, the youngest, was working in the tannery, busily flaying the hide of a mule. He was covered in grease and blood.

Peter told him to just leave off and come as he was. Simon was baling hay when Peter found him in one of the barns.

A good two hours or more had passed by the time all five siblings appeared before Van Driessen and his accountant. Mr. Firth curled his nose at the sight and smell of Tom. But Van Driessen was more sanguine.

"Take the filthy one and get him cleaned up," he said to Peter. Then, addressing Mr. Firth he continued, "We'll have a look at the others in the meantime."

Peter gestured to Tom and the two went back down the road toward the quarters. Mary's shack always had a tub outside, filled and ready for the children's evening bath. Tom would have to use that.

Mary was too old to move around much, but she now had Polly to help with the youngsters. Peter hadn't been told anything, but he knew exactly what was about to happen. All of Sally's children by Tucker were about to be taken away. If that troubled the overseer, Peter didn't care. He only hoped it meant an easier life for the young people.

Polly was sitting on a bench outside Mary's door holding two toddlers, one on each knee. At her feet three more were digging quite seriously in a small pile of dirt.

She brightened immediately at the unusual sight of midday visitors.

"Mista Peter! Tom! How come you here this time a' day?"

Tom and his brothers all lived in the single men's shack now, so Polly rarely saw any of them.

Peter spoke first. "Need t' use ya' tub t' git this one cleaned up. Him an' his brothers an sisters goin t' be leavin' today."

Tom's head jerked round. He'd had no idea what was happening when Peter had summoned him. "Mista Peter, sir. What 'cha mean we leavin'? Where we goin'?"

"Yer goin' with the owner a' this place. He probably takin' ya t' where he live at fer t' be his house servants."

Tom's eyes widened in fear. The idea of leaving the farm was completely incomprehensible. His voice quavered as he asked, "What do a house servant do?"

Peter answered briskly, "Donno. But it don't make no difference. You a smart nigger what learn fast. You be just fine. Now git outta them clothes an' git yerself in that there tub!"

The young man didn't appear much comforted by Peter's words. Nevertheless, he stripped off his filthy clothing – Polly had quickly taken the children inside, closing the door behind her – and climbed into the large barrel-shaped washtub. The water was nearly cold, since Polly hadn't yet heated more in the cauldron Mary kept on the hearth. Tom scrubbed himself clean as best he could and then called out, "Mista Peter! I ain't got nothin else t' put on!"

It was true that the workers had few changes of clothing. Peter had to think quickly; he was fairly certain that it would never occur to the owner whether Tom had any clean clothing to change into. Besides, white men were notoriously short of patience, especially when it came to their slaves. Peter told Tom to stay where he was, then rushed up the road to his own shack. Once inside, Peter pulled out his one good shirt and a pair of flax trousers. The clothing was going to be too small – Tom was much taller than Peter and broader through the chest and shoulders. But they would have to do.

Half an hour later, Peter and Tom had rejoined the others back at Tucker's cabin. Van Driessen had decided that this was, indeed, a fine group of potential servants. He was especially taken with Li'l Mary and Sarah.

"Such a sweet face on this one. Why she's almost as fetching as a white woman! And her sister! Why they could be twins!"

he gushed, walking in circles around the two young women. He freely felt their curls and pinched their cheeks. Taking Sarah by one arm and Li'l Mary by the other, he turned them this way and that, staring quite openly at their breasts and buttocks.

After a moment, he recovered himself and turned to the young men. He examined each one carefully. "I believe they will all do quite nicely," he pronounced at last.

Tucker told Peter to go hitch up one of the plow horses to a buckboard and bring it round to the main road. Silently, all the siblings got in the back and Caesar mounted the front seat, taking up the reins. Van Driessen got up on the driver's seat of his coach and called out to Mr. Firth, "I shall drive the first part and you shall take the second!"

He flicked the reins and the horses took off at a fast trot, the buckboard following.

Peter walked away, while Tucker stood and watched till they were just a cloud of dust in the distance.

CHAPTER 28

*T*he winter following Tucker's children's departure came in colder and snowier than any in recent memory. All outside activity was forced to cease and workers found themselves confined to their shacks, huddled together mostly trying to keep warm.

Unfortunately, the close confinement, coupled with a lack of adequate heat and food led to illness, first among the children. Runny noses gave way to fevers that spiked, no matter how much worried mothers applied poultices or forced down medicinal teas.

In February the first child died, a boy of about ten. In that same month, six more succumbed – all between the ages of six and twelve. Next it was the infants, those six months and older. Every one of them was also dead by the end of the month. In March, the illnesses spread to the young adults; within this group, there was not only scorching fever, but also delirium and a choking cough. Among them, twelve young men and ten girls died.

Because of the bad weather there could be no burials. The dead were simply wrapped up and stacked away from the quarters in one of several open sheds that had been built high on stilts to keep grain safe from foraging animals.

The snows finally let up late in March and the slaves got busy burying their dead. In early April, Tucker and Peter went through the quarters, taking stock of the number of able-bodied workers left. All told, 48 had died. Of those still able to work, there were fewer than 50 hands to tend almost 100 acres. The two men met under a spreading mulberry tree that was just beginning to bud, to assess the situation.

"Ya just gone have t' git some a the older ones out in the field," Tucker announced.

Peter simply stood there, silent. Tucker turned in his direction, apparently waiting for some sort of response. "Well, is there anythin' else ya' kin think t' do?" he asked, peevishly.

"Ya' might ask if'n we kin git us some more slaves," Peter finally offered.

"Goddammit, Nigger!" Tucker exploded, "Ya think I got the right t' tell the owner a' this place t' buy some more? What kinda suggestion is that?"

Almost immediately Tucker regretted his outburst. Peter raised his eyes almost level with the overseer. After a long moment he said, "Well, ya' asked me what I thought an I told ya'."

"Never mind," Tucker said, now shamefaced. "I'll figure somethin' out."

The overseer spent that night turning the problem over in his mind. Or rather, he spent about an hour considering it, during which he drank almost a jug of whisky.

Although Mr. Firth had initially scoffed at his suggestion about adding spirits to the farm's products, the very next month, copper kettles and coils of piping – materials for building a still – arrived on the supply wagon. Now Tucker had access to real whisky and he made sure to keep himself well supplied.

The alcohol kept him company when the solitude of his cabin became too much to bear, especially during the long winter nights. Most times he'd sit in his chair, pulling alternately on his pipe and his jug. Often he wouldn't even bother going to bed, preferring to simply lay his head on the table whenever sleep overcame him.

An idea did come to him, just as dawn was about to break. Why, I do believe Old Mary got a grown-up gal helping her with the babes, he thought. But now, most a' the little niggers on the place is dead. That gal be one more body what can be put in the fields.

Tucker decided to have Peter pass the word to Mary. Meanwhile, he, himself would take another, closer inventory. Any children left alive would have to be pressed into service, even if they were a bit too young. And Old Mary, well if she can still stand up, she gone have t' go too, he decided.

When Tucker broke the news to him about "Mary's grown-up gal" going into the fields, Peter was careful not to register his consternation. For the past twenty years, he and Mary had carefully hidden Polly from the overseer's sight. As the girl had grown to womanhood, she'd become the very image of her mother. This was not a problem in the quarters, since none of the workers had actually seen Sally, at least not up close. But Tucker was another story. There was no way to hide the obvious implications of Polly's resemblance to Sally from him. Still, there was nothing to be done, so Peter simply nodded, as always, and walked away. He decided to stop by Mary's shack that night after the day's work had ended and evening meals were finished. Clearly, the time had finally come for Polly to learn the truth about who she was.

Sally's last child had been the smallest one. Polly had remained so tiny throughout her childhood that everyone always assumed she was younger than her actual age. Like her mother, the girl didn't develop breasts or get her menses until she was almost 15. Now, at twenty, she finally looked like a woman fully grown.

Polly took the news much better than Mary. When Peter told them both that Tucker had ordered Polly to report to the fields the next day, the old woman immediately cried out, covered her face with both hands and sank onto a bench.

"Aint Mary! Why you gittin' so upset? Ain't nothin wrong with me I cain't work the fields!" Polly announced proudly, "I'm big enough an' old enough. An' I kin work a full day just like anybody else!"

"That ain't the problem!" Mary sobbed, "Ain't the problem a'tall! There's somethin' you don't know bout 'cha ma'am an' yer Pa." The old woman was unable to continue.

Peter took up the tale in a monotone, "Yer ma'am were the ovaseer's woman. But yer Pa, well he were one a' the workers. Thing is, the ovaseer don't know nothing 'bout 'cha. Mary an' me, well, we just kept ya' a secret from everybody." He avoided Polly's wide-eyed stare the whole time he was speaking. "What'cha gone have t' do, ya' gone have t' stay outta Masta Tucker sight. Wear one'a the men's hats over yer head rag, so's he cain't see yer face. An', fer Chrissake! Keep yerself covered up!

"I ain't got no men's hat," Polly said, utterly bewildered. What was Mista Peter saying? She'd always been told her mother and a twin had died in childbirth. She knew about the overseer's woman, the woman who was ma'am to Li'l Mary, Sarah, Zack, Simon and Tom. This same woman was her ma'am too? Suddenly, she was angry! "How come ain't nobody never told me before?"

Mary sighed, wiping her eyes with a corner of her apron; she got heavily to her feet. "Chile, you was the one babe yer ma'am wanted more 'n all the others. Sally, yer ma'am, she did love all'a her chil'ren, she did. But, she ain't never had no good feelins fer the ovaseer, they Pa. An' he ain't cared nothing fer none a' them either. But she did love yer Pa, Lemuel, that were his name. Yer ma'am did love him somethin' fierce!"

Polly was fascinated. Her anger forgotten for the moment, she asked, "So, if 'n my ma'am were Masta Tucker woman, how she got me by my pa?"

Both Mary and Peter were silent. Finally, Peter spoke up, "I don't rightly know how she done it, but Sally figured out a way to sneak out an' meet Lemuel. Guess that's when it happened."

"An' where my Pa at now?"

There was another even longer silence, during which Peter and Mary looked at each other, then away. At length, Peter answered flatly, "He dead. Masta Tucker killed him."

"Killed him? Why Masta Tucker done that? You said he ain't know nothing 'bout me." Polly's wide-eyed gaze fixed on Peter's face.

"Masta Tucker did find out bout what'cha ma'am done behind his back 'cause he got t' wonderin' 'bout her and then he kept askin' around. I think yer ma'am must'a done somethin' t'git him riled." Here, Peter paused and glanced uncomfortably toward Mary. After the briefest minute, during which he seemed to come to a decision, he continued with the full story of how he'd discovered the lovers and threatened Sally unless she gave up the trysts.

"Why ya' done that Mista Peter?" Polly asked anxiously.

"Cause they was gone git caught!" Peter exploded. "An' you was borned! I tried t' keep Masta Tucker from findin' out 'bout any of it. I knowed it'd be hard on Sally, havin t' give up her lover, but I reckon that a whole lot better' n having her masta find out 'bout some chile she had by one'a the niggers!"

"Ya see," Mary said hurriedly, "that's why we was so scared fer anybody t' find out about 'cha. No tellin what Masta Tucker do if'n he knowed Sally had a babe what weren't his'n."

"I see," Polly said softly, and, after a beat, "I'm'a do like ya say, Mista Peter. But I still ain't got no hat." She dropped her eyes.

"I'll bring one wit' me in the morning. Just be outside soon as ya hear the horn." Peter said and then took his leave.

Polly whirled around and caught Mary by the hand. "Please, Aint Mary, tell me all about my ma'am an my pa. Do I favor one or 'nother? What was they like? An' why Masta Tucker killed my pa if 'n he ain't know nothing 'bout me? Did somebody tell him bout my pa an my ma'am?"

Mary patted Polly's cheek with her free hand. "Ya got a lotta questions, Chile, but tonight, ya gone need t' git t 'bed. Horn sound real early an' ya need yer sleep. I'm'a tell ya' all about it in time."

Polly slept very little that night. It seemed every time she would doze off, she imagined the summoning blast of the bugle. It was a sound she'd heard her whole life, without ever having to respond to it. Now she feared sleeping through it and having to report late to the fields, an action sure to attract Master Tucker's attention. That was the other reason for her disquiet, the need to remain unnoticed. For Polly was anything but. Everyone seemed to have become aware of her, wherever she went in the quarters. She couldn't say what had changed, but, ever since she'd become a woman, the eyes of most every male worker seemed to follow her, no matter whether she was drawing water, fetching firewood, or on some other errand for Mary. She'd asked Mary why this was so.

"Poor chile, ya' ain't never seen yerself, have ya'. Yer a real pretty gal, is what. The menfolk do like t 'look on pretty gals. Don't 'cha worry 'bout it none."

And so Polly had learned to take it all in stride. But now suddenly she had to make herself well nigh invisible and she wasn't sure how to manage that. Before dawn, she finally gave up trying to sleep. Getting up as quietly as she could, she dressed in several layers of loose clothing and wrapped her head, tying the cloth tightly at the nape of her neck. Then she waited by the door for the horn. At the first blast, she slipped outside and joined the knot of people gathering in the clearing.

Peter was standing a little apart from the others, holding the bugle. For the last fifteen years or so, he'd been the one blowing the summons to start the workday. It was the only way to get everyone out at daybreak, since Tucker was most often absent until late morning or even early afternoon. As soon as he spotted Polly, Peter approached her and handed her a wide-brimmed straw hat.

"Keep this pulled down so's yer face stay hid," he ordered, "An' member t' keep yer head down, 'specially when the ovaseer come round."

The work crews headed out to their various assignments. Peter kept Polly in the group he was leading, figuring that Tucker would spend his time in another field, once he finally showed himself.

Peter spent that first morning showing Polly how to swing her scythe so as to cleanly cut the sheaves of wheat without injuring herself in the process. The young woman struggled mightily, trying to control the heavy, long handled implement.

By noon, Polly was drenched in sweat and about to faint from the heat. "I gotta take off some'a these clothes," she thought. Looking around to make sure nobody was nearby, she shed the extra blouse she'd put on, undid her apron and took off the extra skirt. She made a neat bundle of the clothing and then searched for a place to hide it until sundown. She found a stump of a tree trunk close to the edge of the field and placed her bundle behind the stump.

Just as she was about to return to the row where she'd been working, she spotted someone on horseback coming in her direction. Polly quickly ducked behind a row of uncut wheat and scurried back to her spot. Picking up the scythe, she began whacking away furiously.

The rest of that first day passed with no further sightings of the overseer. Polly made it her business to stay close to Peter until nightfall. If he noticed that she'd removed some of her clothing, he said nothing about it. When he finally blew the horn signaling the end of work, Polly returned to the tree stump, only to find her bundle missing. Frightened now, she hurried to catch up with the last of the workers leaving the field. Peter had lingered behind and he intercepted her.

"Thought I told ya t ' keep out 'a sight. Why ya' back here all by yerself?"

"Mista Peter, I taken off some'a my clothes when I got hot, an' hid them behind a tree stump. But when I went back, they wasn't there."

Peter frowned, then asked, "Anybody see ya?

"There were this man on horseback. I think he seen me," Polly answered hesitantly.

"Goddammit!" Peter muttered, "Goddammit!" Then he took hold of Polly's shoulder and hustled her back to the quarters. At Mary's door, he finally released his grip.

"Ya' ain't gone be workin' tomorrow," he ordered. "Want'cha t 'stay outta sight fer a few days. Don't even come outside till everybody gone t'the fields."

CHAPTER 29

It seemed to Tucker as though he'd forgotten what rest felt like. In spite of the fact that he was barely working a full day, he couldn't for the life of him relax enough to stay asleep for a full night. No matter how much he drank, how drunk he got, after the first few hours, sleep eluded him. This always made his mornings impossible. He'd begin the day so tired that he'd have to literally drag himself out of bed – if in fact he ever made it to bed.

The years had not made him any more introspective, so he'd never acknowledged the depths of his grief and disappointment at the cruel turn his life had taken. And therefore, he'd remained stuck, unable even to contemplate taking another woman. Part of the lure of drink was how it kept him from feeling the almost unendurable pain of losing Sally.

On this particular day, as his horse was ambling from one field to another, Tucker just happened to glance into the wheat field where a woman was taking off her blouse. Curious, the overseer reined his horse to a stop and watched as she took off her apron and stepped out of her skirt. Tucker was surprised to see that the woman was still fully dressed; she'd been wearing extra clothes! It was at this point that the overseer forgot the incongruity of anyone being so covered up on such a hot day; the woman's body was *lovely*! The homespun frock she wore couldn't conceal perfectly formed arms and limbs, nor the tiny waist and shockingly wide hips. The girl had Sally's body!

"Oh my God! She come back!" Tucker actually spoke aloud. He spurred his horse in the direction of the young woman, only to discover that she had vanished. Slowing to a walk, he made his way to the spot where he'd first seen her. He got down and searched around the tree stump. He found the bundle of clothing but could not locate the owner. Tucker walked up and down every row, searching. Each time he stopped near a woman, he would show her the bundle. And since he had no sensible question to ask her other than, "You know whose clothes these is?" she would simply stare at him in confusion. Finally, he gave up and returned to his horse. "My mind playin tricks on me," he decided. "Maybe I need to cut out some'a the drinkin'." Still, the bundle of clothing was real enough, even if he had imagined the woman was Sally.

Maybe that was it; maybe it was time for him to have a woman again. "After all, I ain't gittin' no younger," he mused. "Just gotta be careful not t 'git so attached this time." Whoever it was who owned the bundle of clothing, well she might just be a good place to start looking.

At first Tucker considered asking Peter about this mysterious woman, but then decided against it. Even if Peter knew who those clothes belonged to, Tucker was sure the man wouldn't tell him the truth. So he decided instead to approach Mary. But he wasn't sure she would be of any help either.

After considering and then discarding the idea of asking first one, then another slave, the overseer had to finally conclude that even the fear of punishment wasn't enough for any of them to give him trustworthy information about one of their own. This realization put a halt to his investigations, at least for the next few weeks.

Yet the bundle of clothing taunted him. He'd brought them back to his cabin and placed them in a corner next to the hearth.

Each evening, he'd glance at them just before getting out his jug. Once the alcohol began to work its magic, creating hazy, uncontrollable thoughts, Tucker's mind would conjure up scenes of Sally. Sally drawing water from his well. Sally stirring a stew over the fire. Sally, big with child, walking slowly across his floor. Always, Sally. Even drinking now gave him no relief! He had to find the owner of those clothes. Finally he decided he'd just have to begin by asking Mary.

Mary, now somewhere in her fifties, bore the distinction of being the oldest woman on the farm. And, even though Tucker had summoned her into the fields, severely arthritic hands and knees made it nearly impossible for her to do even half a day's work. So Peter made sure to assign her to one of his own work gangs, where he could keep an eye on her. At the first sign of weariness, he always sent her back to the quarters immediately.

There was no need, he felt, to get Tucker's permission beforehand. And therefore, this was where she spent most of her days, sitting on a three-legged stool by the door to her shack. Once Peter had determined that it was safe for Polly to return to the fields, Mary would wait here for her return at day's end.

And so, this was where Tucker found her, after searching the fields for several days in a row.

"Thought you was supposed t' be out workin'," the overseer began, but then changed tack. "There was a bundle a' clothes left out in the rye field a couple weeks ago. You know who they belongs to?"

Mary squinted up at him. "Masta Tucker, ain't nobody 'round here got no clothes t' be throwin' away. You sure they belongs t' one a' us?"

For just a moment, Tucker actually considered the logic of what she was saying. Then he remembered who he was dealing with.

"I'm a find out 'bout these clothes from somebody," he muttered. Then, louder, "By the way, where that near-grown gal ya been keeping? Told Peter she gotta start workin' the fields too."

"Why she out there now, Masta. Couldn't rightly say where she at, but she workin', Masta, fer sure."

Suddenly, Tucker had an absolutely brilliant idea. "Well, day's end, when she git back, tell her t' git herself up t' my cabin. I'm'a git a good look at her fer myself." He ended on a triumphant note, turned on his heel and was about to leave. "I expect that gal at my door come nightfall. You see t' it!" He headed up the road that led back to the fields.

Mary sat stock still. This was disastrous! All the years of lies and hiding, trying to protect this innocent child – it was all coming undone! "Cain't let this happen!" she said as she heaved herself to her feet and started up the road. She couldn't think of any way to protect Polly but maybe Peter could.

Fortunately, Mary knew exactly where to find Peter, and therefore, Polly. Today, they were harvesting wheat. It was possible that Tucker might be there too, but Mary knew she had to take that chance.

She reached the field huffing and puffing. Without stopping to catch her breath, she headed up one row and down the next until she found Peter working right beside Polly. Mary caught him by the shoulders, forcing him to straighten up and lower his scythe.

"Masta Tucker come t' find me just now. He sayin' he wanna see Polly tonight! I gotta send her t' his cabin soon as work finish! Peter! What we gone do?"

Polly was standing right behind Peter. Somehow, she knew neither Mary nor Peter would be able to protect her now. "Aint

Mary. Mista Peter. Think I know how t' take care a' this," she said somewhat hesitantly.

Peter turned to face her, the anguish in his eyes spilling over into his voice. "Gal, ya don't know what' cha talkin' 'bout. Ya look too much like yer ma'am! An' I know, fer a fact, that man doted on that gal more' n any white man should a nigger! No tellin' what he do t' ya!"

Polly lifted her chin. A peculiar smile pulled at the corners of her mouth. She spoke softly, but firmly. "You both done all ya could fer as long as ya could. I'm'a have t' protect my own self now." She picked up her scythe and headed out of the field. Peter hurried after her.

"Gal!" he shouted, "where ya goin?"

She turned back briefly. "Please don' foller me. I'll be back directly." She disappeared into a copse of trees at the edge of the wheat field.

Polly walked for what could have been miles, completely oblivious to either the passage of time or fatigue. It was as though her body had detached itself from her spirit. When, at last she stopped in a small clearing, she became aware of the scythe still clutched in her right hand.

Stretching out her left arm, she drew the blade along its length, marveling at the bubbling line of red. She drew more lines in that arm, then moved to her shoulder. Amazingly, she could feel no pain, only an overwhelming need to cut, cut everywhere!

Polly shifted the scythe to her left hand so as to slice her right arm. She used the blade on both legs, thighs to ankles, cutting, endlessly cutting. Finally, she drew the point of the blade down the length of her cheek, from just below her left eye to under her chin; she stopped just short of cutting her own throat. Blood soaked her sleeves and her skirts, ran down her legs and made a puddle around her bare feet.

The sun had moved to the mid-afternoon position by the time Polly returned to the wheat field. As she emerged from the cover of trees, one of the women spotted her and screamed. Everyone dropped whatever work he or she was doing and ran to investigate. The workers surrounded the girl, now bleeding profusely. Several shouted to Peter to "Go fetch Masta Tucker!"

Tucker had been circling the fields on horseback when he heard the screaming and shouting. He spurred his horse to a gallop and almost ran Peter down on the road between fields. Tucker called out, "What's all that noise about?"

"One'a the gals cut herself! She cut real bad!" Peter gasped, shock nearly stealing his voice.

"What' cha mean she cut herself? How you let that happen? Wasn't ya watchin'?"

Peter stared at Tucker as though he'd never seen the man before. Realization was setting in slowly, calming him, allowing him to think about what he wanted to say next.

"Masta Tucker, sir, I do believe this gal gone daft! She took off into the woods an' done the cuttin' in secret. Ain't nobody seen her till she come back!"

Tucker didn't even hear Peter's full response. He'd dug his spurs into the horse's sides before Peter was half finished. Reaching the wheat field, he reined and dismounted almost in a single movement. Polly was standing in the center of a group of women, each one trying to staunch her many wounds. The overseer strode into their midst, pushing several aside.

"Gal!" he demanded. "Who all cut 'cha up like that?"

Polly gave him that strange, slightly unfocused smile. "Oh, Masta. Ya know, whilst I was workin', somethin' just come over me an' I done it t' myself." Polly held out both arms toward the overseer. "See, Masta, ain't it pretty?" She reached down and lifted her bloody skirts, baring her mutilated legs. "See that!"

she proclaimed proudly, "I ain't stopped cuttin' till I 's runnin' blood!"

Tucker backed away. Who was this girl? It took him a few minutes to recognize her as the one he'd been searching for, the one who'd hidden the clothes. He'd been ready to make her his new woman! But now, here she was, obviously quite mad!

"One a ya need t' take a hold a' this here gal an' lock her up!" Tucker shouted at no one in particular. Still backing up, he nearly stumbled into his horse. He turned grabbed the saddle's pommel, mounted and galloped off. Out on the main road, Tucker nearly collided with the supply wagon. He'd completely forgotten that today was the first of the month.

"Hallo!" he called out to the teamster at the reins. "I'm'a need yer help transportin' a slave what's gone mad. Think ya' kin take her back t' Albany?"

The driver shifted the reins to one hand; with the other, he scratched his chin whiskers. "We cain't be transportin' no mad slaves. We gotta keep t' our schedule. But, 'bout a half a league from here, there's a wagon full a' slaves bound fer New York City.

They's a rough lot, bad workers an' runaways what they masters wanted t' git rid of. If'n ya want, ya kin try an' catch up wit' them whilst we unloadin' and collectin' yer goods."

Tucker took off in the direction the driver had pointed, leaving the teamsters to fend for themselves. After all, this crew knew they had to find Peter first in order to get anything else done. Tucker rode hard for the better part of an hour before he spotted the wagon some distance ahead. When he got within hailing distance, he started shouting and waving his hat.

Two white men sat in front, one driving while the other carried a whip and a flintlock. In the wagon were about 30 or so chained and manacled men, both young and mature, along with four obviously older women. In a group like this, the older men and women were mostly just too worn-out for their masters to continue feeding them. Only the young men were likely to have been runners.

Mostly these slaves had belonged to small farmers who could neither afford to keep the old or sick nor effectively punish runaways. Such slaves were routinely sold to traveling slave merchants who would then resell them in the bustling New York slave markets for transport to the southern Colonies.

The wagon driver didn't immediately hear Tucker's shout, but the other man did and nudged the driver until he got his attention. Tucker gallopped and caught up. As he approached, he noticed that the man holding the gun and whip had only one eye. The hole where the other eye should have been was covered with a black patch that was completely sunken in, as though the entire eyeball had been snatched out of his skull. The sight so completely unnerved Tucker that it took the overseer a full minute to recover enough to make his request.

"I got a woman on the farm I work at what's gone daft. She cut herself up when nobody was lookin', so she need t' be off the place 'fore night fall. No tellin' what she might do next."

One-Eye, his single pale blue orb unblinking, studied Tucker carefully. When he finally spoke, he had a voice that invoked dry bones in a charnel house. "What makes you think we'd be interested in your mad nigger wench? We can't sell her if she's as daft, as you say."

Tucker could feel himself growing desperate. In his mind's eye, he could still see Polly, her bleeding arms outstretched, reaching toward him. In that moment, he realized that he couldn't stay on any farm where that sort of madness could seize someone, seemingly out of the blue. For the first time, he truly feared that a similar madness was stalking him too.

"Listen, I'm willin' t' give the woman to ya. Just take her off the place an' ya kin do whatever ya want with her. I don't care!"

"You're the overseer, right? By whose authority are you giving a worker away that doesn't belong to you?" One-Eye's funereal diction was becoming more perfect, the longer he spoke.

Tucker hesitated, but only for a moment before saying, "I'm doin' the owner a' the place a favor, gittin' rid a' this woman. Sides," he continued morosely, "I done supplied him with five others over the years."

One-Eye nodded to the driver who circled the wagon around and followed Tucker to the farm.

Back in the wheat field, everyone was thoroughly confused as to what to do next; they all still stood in a circle around Polly. As soon as he reached them Peter gestured to Mary, who stepped forward and gingerly took Polly by the arm.

"Chile, ya gotta come wit me now. Lemme git 'cha cleaned up." Mary gently led Polly back to the quarters. Her cuts would have to be washed and dressed to keep them from festering. Once inside, the old woman faced her young charge.

"Whatever got into you, hurtin' yerself like ya done!" she fussed, "What was ya thinking? These cuts is gone heal up bad! Big ol' scars, that's what 'cha gone have…all over!" All the while as she spoke, Mary was busily soaking a clean cloth in water from her kettle and wiping off the now-drying blood from Polly's face and arms. Then, she made the young woman take off her skirt so she could do the same for Polly's legs.

"Oh Aint Mary, I know that," Polly said wincing from the pain she was now beginning to feel. "I just knowed I weren't gone do like my ma'am. I weren't gone let that man take me an' give me no passel a' babes what didn't belong t' me!"

"Well, I guess ya done that, all right. Don't think he'll want 'cha now."

"Aint Mary." Polly said suddenly, "Ya ain't never told me why Masta Tucker killed my pa. Did Mista Peter tell on my pa? That why?"

Mary kept wetting her cloth and wiping away blood. After several silent moments, she finally answered. "No, it weren't Mista Peter told. It were yer pa what confessed so's Masta Tucker wouldn't beat everybody, just him. Masta Tucker, well he used the old ovaseer's whip instead a' the one he use regular. That whippin' were the worst thing I ever seen! Tore yer pa's back up! Taken the flesh off the bones, what it done!" Overcome with the memory, Mary's voice choked up.

"Thing nobody ever could figger out, why yer pa never hollered, never made not one sound the whole time. Masta Tucker never stop a whippin' till a nigger start in hollerin'. Yer pa never made not one sound, so Masta Tucker just beat him t' death."

Polly was silent through the rest of Mary's ministrations. The old woman's words settled into the young woman's heart. "I'm'a make sure that man send me off this farm today," she told herself. She stepped into her bloodied skirt, pulled it up and fastened it round her waist. Then she pulled on her stained blouse and headed for the door.

"Chile! Where ya goin'?" Mary cried out, aghast. "I told ya them cuts is gone fester if' n they ain't cleaned up proper!"

"Sorry Aint Mary, I gotta git back t' the fields. You done more'n yer share a' runnin' round today. Yer limbs is gone hurt too much tonight." Polly turned around and hugged Mary hard. "I ain't never gone forget'cha, what you an' Mista Peter done fer me. Not never." She gave the old woman an extra squeeze and left her standing in the doorway.

About that same time, the teamsters reached the farm's main road. One went to find Peter while the other, the driver, took a brief rest in the wagon. Once Peter was located, he oversaw the transfer of provisions into the barns and the loading of produce for market. Just as they were finishing up, Tucker arrived followed by the slavers' wagon. He immediately demanded to know where "that mad wench was at."

Peter stopped directing the work long enough to level a baleful stare at the overseer. Then, he walked off silently, heading in the direction of the quarters. Tucker was about to shout after him when Polly suddenly appeared on the road. She stopped in front of Peter, just for a moment before continuing up the road toward the overseer. Once she got abreast of the slave merchants wagon, she began grinning and twisting herself about. Again, she extended her arms, and then raised her skirts, covered with now-drying blood.

Tucker could sense a deep terrifying void opening up in his soul. "See what I was tellin' ya!" he shouted, "That nigger woman be a danger t' everybody 'round here! No tellin' what got into her!"

One-Eye coolly observed the scene. Yes, it did appear that the woman had gone mad, which made the prospect of trying to sell her quite slim. The man offered an observation and a suggestion. "The madness may prove more of a passing thing than a permanent condition. Why don't you just tie her up in one of the barns and see whether she gets better with time?"

"No!" Tucker screamed, "I cain't have no mad woman on no farm where I'm at! Take her! Just take her off the place!"

"Suit yourself, then." One-Eye sighed, and picked up a length of rope from the wagon floor. Getting down, he approached Polly carefully, his head cocked to one side so as to keep his lone eye on her. As soon as he got within striking distance, he sprang forward and pounced on the girl, knocking her to the ground. He turned her on her stomach and quickly used the rope to hog-tie her, wrists and ankles. Now properly restrained, he could easily pick Polly up and carry her to the wagon.

But Polly offered no resistance whatsoever; as soon as the man attacked her, she went limp and stayed that way. Once in the wagon, she righted herself and quietly squeezed herself between two of the women who were sitting close to the back. No one looked directly at Polly. One-Eye, as soon as he was satisfied that she wasn't going to make a commotion, went back upfront and climbed up onto the seat. He nudged the driver and the wagon took off at a smart clip.

Polly watched the farm retreating as the horses picked up speed. At last, she could draw breath without fearing someone might notice and single her out. No one was looking at her now. The two women on either side kept their eyes carefully averted. Polly glanced down at her arms and realized her wounds were still oozing. Fresh damp patches of red were starting to spread on her skirts. And now the pain had become intense and burning. Just as her tears were about to fall, one of the women maneuvered her manacled hand just enough to touch Polly.

"Don't'cha worry none," the woman whispered, "When we's stopped fer the night, I'm'a take care a' them cuts fer ya."

The driver kept the horses moving at a good speed. After a spell, he ventured a glance toward the back of the wagon. "Meester," he said, "that mad one, she got right quiet back there, yah?" The man's accent was so thick that his English sounded exactly like his native Dutch.

One-Eye glanced behind himself as well. "Well," he observed, "I did tell that overseer fellow she'd quiet down in a spell. These poor ignorant louts are no smarter than the slaves. At any rate, we got ourselves a perfectly good wench for nothing! She'll fetch a fair price if one just wants a field hand. It won't really matter what she looks like."

CHAPTER 30

*E*vening gathered stealing the light from every corner of the farm, enveloping fields and structures till all were blanketed in darkness. Workers in their shacks took their meals, did small chores and then fell asleep on corn-husk mattresses or on blankets spread out on dirt floors.

Back in his cabin, even as the room grew increasingly dark, Tucker was still rooting around under piles of debris, searching for his whisky jug. He seldom bothered even to light a fire, other than when he simply had to, preferring to get by with the light from a single candle. After all, nothing was ever moved now; he could always find exactly what he needed. Tonight, he truly needed to get as drunk as possible.

"Here 'tis," he muttered, finally unearthing the jug and getting to his feet. In tipping the thing to his lips, he nearly fell over backward, momentarily quite dizzy.

"Dammit!" he said aloud, "I ain't even taken one sip! I cain't be drunk already!"

Tucker stumbled to his chair and sat heavily, placing his candlestick on the edge of the table nearby. The spell passed as quickly as it had come on him and he took a long swallow from the jug. The liquid, warm and faintly sweet, began to work its magic almost immediately.

The unsettling events of the day, still so sharply etched in his mind began to grow fuzzy at the edges. After a few more pulls on the jug, he could no longer see *that woman's bloody arms* reaching out for him. He continued to drink until the jug was empty, at which point he tried to set it in exactly the same spot occupied by the still burning candle.

Tucker didn't notice that in placing the jug, he'd knocked the candle and its holder onto the floor. His head lolled back and then sank forward until his chin was resting on his chest. Within minutes he was snoring.

Peter couldn't sleep. After all those years of anxiety over keeping Sally's daughter a secret, it was impossible to believe she was finally safe from discovery. Peter found himself wondering where she was going and what would happen to her now, especially since she had mutilated herself so badly. His mind then wondered to her mother – and her father.

Had he never confronted Sally over the affair, what would have happened? Would Lemuel still be alive? Would Sally, herself have lived? Strange to be worrying about all that now, Peter realized. But in the darkness, with this unfamiliar sense of freedom, he couldn't seem to control his thoughts.

Finally, he got up from the narrow mattress he now used. The larger bed he'd given to Lucy and the man she'd finally decided on as her husband, a decent enough fellow, quiet and willing to follow Peter's lead in most things. They all shared the shack now. Peter had set his bed near the door, since he had to be up before everyone else. Lucy and Henrik – that was the husband's name – slept in the back, their bed against the rear wall.

As soon as his feet hit the floor, Peter realized that something else had gotten his attention. There was a peculiar reddish glow visible through the front window. When he opened the door, he could make out that the light was just beyond the line of trees separating the workers' quarters from the main road.

Peter went back inside and pulled on his shoes. Without waking anyone else, he slipped out and headed in the direction of the light. As he reached the road leading up to the overseer's cabin, he now could make out the lurid glow. Tucker's place was completely engulfed in flames!

Peter stopped dead, his brain trying to comprehend what to do. Of course, he should sound an alarm; get a water brigade together and put out the flames. Maybe Tucker had been able to out before the fire got too far along. The overseer might be lying outside somewhere in need of assistance.

Yet Peter didn't make a move toward the cabin. Instead, he stood watching the flames, picturing his three children, forever lost to him – and Lucy, who wouldn't have had to die in childbirth if she weren't only trying to replace that loss.

Tucker had done nothing but cause him misery! It didn't matter that the overseer never realized it. Peter understood how the man's mind worked, always had. Silently, he turned and headed back to the quarters. Apparently, no one else had seen the fire, so there would be no need for him to justify not attempting a rescue.

Just after daybreak, the skies opened up and poured rain. Then there came repeated claps of thunder accompanied by frequent lightning strikes. Stormy days usually meant no field work. And, if there were indoor chores, then either Peter or Tucker would usually assign them specifically.

Today, however, workers waited in their shacks as the morning wore on and the rain fell in sheets. Finally, in the early afternoon, there were breaks in the downpours and several people ventured outside. They gathered in front of Peter's shack. One man knocked hesitantly on the door. When there was no response, he pushed it open. There was no one inside.

"Hallo?" he called out, surveying the empty room. "Peter, where ya' at?"

"Maybe he over by Mary's," another offered.

The small group trouped down the road to Mary's shack. When they got within hailing distance, Mary called out from her open front door. "If'n ya lookin' fer Peter, he gone. Him an' his family done left outta here sometime 'fore sunrise. He say t' tell alla ya' the ovaseer dead – burnt up in a fire at his cabin. You kin go look fer his body if'n ya' wanna bury him. But Peter say if'n ya' smart you'll do like he done an' git away from here fore anybody fine out what happened. The sooner ya' leave, the farther you'll git."

By now, Quash had joined the group. He stepped to the front, essentially taking control of the conversation. "How come he ain't tell nobody what happened 'cept you?"

Mary folded her arms across her bosom. "Now Quash," she began gently, "You ain't the first person I'd tell if'n I was plannin' on runnin'. When you ever been able to keep quiet 'bout anything?"

"That ain't the point!" Quash sputtered. "Anyhow, why he leave you behind if'n he taken' his daughter an' Henrik?"

"I'm too old an' lame t' do no runnin'. Figgered I'll just stay put till the owner fine out what happened an' send in a new ovaseer. Alla you kin decide fer yerselves what' cha wanna do. I done sent off four a' my sons an' they families. Luke an' his family say they gone stay here wit' me."

The storm clouds lifted and a bright afternoon sun spread warming rays over the countryside. There was more than enough produce in the several barns to divide up for each of the departing families. Men and women had little in the way of personal belongings so everyone could travel light. People left singly and in small groups. By late afternoon, the farm was all but deserted.

CHAPTER 31

*I*t should have taken only one month for conditions on Van Driessen's farm to come to the attention of the owner in Albany. After all, the first-of-the-month supply wagon did reach the farm as scheduled. The teamsters spent several hours wandering through the deserted structures where untended cows lowed more miserably than ever and in the several chicken coops, the few skinny birds that had been left behind scratched and pecked listlessly. When it became clear that neither Tucker nor Peter was anywhere to be found in the usual places, one of the teamsters suggested checking the overseer's cabin.

A heavy odor still hung over the burned wreckage. Several more days of steady rain throughout the month had created a sodden mess of blackened carbonized wood, twisted metal and ash. Tucker's body and the chair he died in had been so thoroughly incinerated that one was indistinguishable from the other or from the rest of the ruined cabin.

The teamsters, quite shaken by now, decided to leave the place without making an attempt to locate anyone else. Since it had never been their habit to go anyplace near the slave quarters, it didn't cross anyone's mind to check them now. The men simply hurried back to the supply wagon and headed directly back to Albany fully intending to make a complete report.

Unfortunately, circumstances made delivering that report impossible. Neither Petrus Van Driessen III nor his accountant was available when the teamsters reached Albany. Petrus and his fiancee had married in the month following his only visit to the farm. And in the midst of the whirl of balls and celebrations leading up to the wedding, Jason Firth had fallen ill. The accountant died two days following the nuptuals. Not ones to let any such unpleasantness dampen their joyous occasion, the newlyweds left Albany as planned for a monthlong series of visits with relatives who hadn't been able to come to the wedding.

That visit stretched into a second month. As a result, fully three months passed before Petrus was made aware of the events on his most profitable farm. The losses in livestock and produce were bad enough, but the loss of over forty-five slaves was nearly incalculable. For the first time in two generations, the Van Driessen family fortune suffered a decline from which it would never fully recover.

Nonetheless, Van Driessen and his new bride established themselves on the family estate. Their entire retinue of slaves included Li'l Mary and Sarah, who were now expected to keep the house clean and running smoothly, as well as Zack, Simon and Tom, whose duties included upkeep of the grounds and maintaining the several carriages and horses. Li'l Mary and her siblings understood the rhythm of farming, cutting, baling, milking and gathering, tasks requiring hard physical work. The three young men easily adapted to their new and considerably easier duties. To the two sisters, however, housekeeping was entirely alien. What did one do with feather dusters or feather beds? How could a body be expected to clean a delicate piece of porcelain without having the thing leap off its shelf and shatter itself into bits? Van Driessen had no older experienced servant who could guide his novices; the task would have to fall to his bride, herself little more than a girl and younger by several years than the youngest of Sally's children.

But Peter had noted, quite correctly, that Sally's children were all "smart niggers what learn quick." Li'l Mary especially proved quite adept if not at the fine points of cleaning, then at least at keeping her mistress from noticing tasks only half done. Sarah followed her sister's lead and, together they convinced Mistress Van Driessen that she was absolutely in charge and that everything was in order. Mistress easily convinced Master of the same.

In fact, Van Driessen, ever the optimist and now without the prudent guiding hand of his father's accountant, refused to burden himself with worries about either the decrease in the size of his fortune or how successfully his wife supervised their servants. After all, he, himself was more than satisfied with the prospect of having his two quite comely house slaves potentially at his beck and call. Potential however does not assure actuality. Li'l Mary made sure that her mistress knew her and her sister's whereabouts at all times. And, without having to overtly frustrate Master Van Driessen's clumsy attempts to get one or the other alone, Li'l Mary and Sarah were able to remain as virginal as they'd been when they left the farm. In fact, their ploy worked so well that both sisters managed to consign themselves to permanent slave spinsterhood. No man would ever know either of them. If Master Van Driessen could not impregnate them himself, he was completely disinclined to purchase males to serve the purpose, even if it might have increased his number of slaves. Babies of house slaves were worthless until they grew old enough to put to work. He wouldn't have minded his own slave offspring but he could not abide the thought of anyone elses.

The three brothers, however, were another matter entirely. Zack, Simon and Tom would indeed fetch good prices as stud Negroes on the farms of the Van Driessens' neighbors. Mistress

Van Driessen didn't like the idea at first but her husband was finally able to convince her by pointing out that male slaves were different in that they *needed* to breed. Moreover, each transaction could bring in a hefty cash return that would increase the Van Driessen coffers.

Sally and Tucker's line would continue through her sons.

CHAPTER 32

For Polly, the wagon trip down to New York meant days and nights that bled together. The incessant jostling made her so sick that she was unable to swallow her share of the hard tack the slavers distributed to their cargo each evening. The woman who had tended her wounds on the first night tried offering the young woman herbs from the stash she'd managed to secret in one of her apron pockets but nothing seemed to ease Polly's nausea. As the days wore on she became thinner, her clothes hanging more and more loosely on her tiny frame.

The route south to New York City took two weeks, since the slavers made several more stops at farms in an effort to purchase or otherwise obtain a few more slaves. They weren't successful, so the wagon, already crowded, didn't become more so. They reached Spuyten Duyvil Creek on a Sunday evening, just after the King's Bridge toll-taker had closed his booth and left for the night. This meant yet another delay.

By the time they finally reached the High Road to Boston, which was the main road into the city, all the slaves were in need of cleaning and fattening up. The wagon skirted the Commons and turned south onto Broad Way, One-Eye and his companion drove to a warehouse near the East River where a number of slave pens were located. Here, the factors or auctioneers arranged the slave auctions that were held in different locations around the city almost daily. Two of these factors, partners of the slavers, took charge of the thirty-five black men and women, separating them into groups of five. Each group was stripped naked, washed roughly and redressed, the men in burlap trousers and the women in burlap shifts that barely reached their knees. They were all herded onto a wooden platform raised just above the crowd of potential buyers, thereby allowing a full view of each slave as he or she was put up for sale.

Polly was placed with the last group. A black man, who was in charge of keeping the groups in order, glanced at her briefly and shuddered before shoving her into place at the end of the line. By now, her cuts had scabbed over, but the scars on her arms and legs gleamed, a shiny pink mosaic of lines. And on her face, a long pink line bisected her left cheek. She watched the man's back as he walked away, then looked down at her arms and legs, trying to see what had so repulsed him. It don't matter what he think, she decided, these scars got me free a' the ovaseer. Don't care what happen now. The group she'd been placed with was moving along briskly.

Cicero had been coming to the docks to watch the slave auctions for years, usually after finishing work running a ferry service between New York City and Long Island. He would always make sure to stay well away from the crowd of whites, mostly men, and the few black servants trusted enough by their masters to purchase or rent one or two additions to the household staff. Cicero, however, was free – had been ever since the white ferryman who'd owned him retired, emancipated him and gave him the business. Over the years, he'd been putting aside whatever money he didn't need to pay the men who manned the boats with him or for upkeep. His savings now totaled a little over £50. He scanned the groups of shackled men and women, as he always did taking in the details of each face. He was never sure what brought him to these auctions or why he felt compelled to study the slaves on sale so closely. Today, as soon as his eye fell on Polly, something moved inside him. Easing carefully around the edges of the crowd, he approached the back of the platform, where the black man handling the groups was standing. He gestured to get the man's attention.

"How much fer the woman got all a' them scars?"

"Who ya buyin' her fer?"

"Fer myself."

The man turned and walked away, returning a few moments later. "Ya kin have the wench fer £50 sterling, paid on takin' possession."

"I'm a' go git the money. Don' let her go 'fore I git back."

"Best t' hurry. They ain't gone hold up the sale fer no nigger."

Cicero took off at a dead run, heading for his house, which was adjacent to the ferry landing. Once there, he lifted a floor board and pulled out a leather sack containing every cent he'd managed to save. Clutching the sack to his breast, he ran the whole way back, managing to reach the platform just as Polly was about to be put up for sale. He gestured to the black handler, holding up the sack so the man could see that he had brought the money. The man took it and, without otherwise acknowledging him, turned and disappeared. Returning a few minutes later, he said, "Wait over there, out the way." He pointed to a spot well back of the crowd.

The woman just ahead of Polly sold in only five minutes and was pulled out of the line. Polly was next in line to be sold. In spite of her insistence that she didn't care what happened to her now, Polly found herself shaking. Suddenly, the black man reappeared, grabbed her arm and yanked her away from the group. Eyes still averted, he pushed her ahead of him toward some wooden steps at the end of the platform. At the top of the steps, he removed her manacles.

"G'on now. Ya been sold."

Polly stared at the man, then turned toward the direction he was pointing. A lone black man stood there, some distance from the white buyers. He wore a hat that shaded his face, but Polly could see he was dressed in rough homespun shirt and pants, woolen socks and heavy shoes. Fascinated and more than a little frightened, she walked toward the man. As she got closer, she could see that he was a head taller than she and quite lean – a man accustomed to hard labor. When they were finally face to face, Polly dropped her eyes, waiting to be told what to do next. There was a long silence before he finally spoke. "You free now," he told her.

There was another even longer silence during which Polly dared not even breathe. Free – what could this man be saying? At last she stammered a question.

"Mista, what'cha mean I'm free?"

"I bought ya an' now I'm 'a free ya. You ain't gotta obey no-body no more. You a free woman."

Polly's legs gave way and she fell to her knees, so overcome she could'nt say another word. Tears filling her eyes, she grabbed both the man's hands and kissed them repeatedly. Finally she was able to cry out, "Oh Mista, you have surely saved my life! Oh thank you! You my savior!"

The man appeared embarrassed as he eased first one hand then the other out of her grasp and helped her to her feet. "Ya ain't got t' call me mister," he stammered. "Name's Cicero. I know you ain't got no place t'stay at right now. If'n you want, ya kin stay in my house. I kin fix ya up a place what's private. An' I'm a God-fearin' Christian man; ya ain't gone have no cause t' worry 'bout me."

At these words, Polly raised her eyes to meet his and she felt her heartbeat skip, then settle into an unfamiliar rhythm. A peculiar energy surged through her, lighting up her eyes and loosening her tongue. As they walked away from the slave market she told him her name and began to tell her story. The afternoon sun poured out its gold over the narrow gabled rooftops and crowded streets.